# SILENCE
## OF
# THE NIGHT

*By*

## Sandra Rowell

Published by

**Cauliay Publishing & Distribution**
PO Box 12076
Aberdeen
AB16 9AL
www.cauliaybooks.com

**First Edition**
**ISBN 978-0-9564624-4-2**
Copyright © Sandra Rowell 2010
Cover design by Michael Molden © Cauliay Publishing

# Acknowledgments

To Mike & Elaine, for your continued friendship and support, without you guys I would not have made it this far. Also, to my friends and family, who have kept my feet firmly on the ground, and given me the confidence to continue my dream. Finally I would like to thank Cauliay Publishing, for having faith in me and my work.

# Preface

A deep impenetrable silence that splits the night in two; a silence that allows lovers to dream of carefree laughter on some tropical shore, a silence that grows in the imagination of a city financier into the hustle and bustle of the stock exchange, that is how the night is or should be, but that is not the way it always is. In your dark silence you take a look down strange alleyways that crisscross every town and city and you see things that should not be seen, shadows that creep menacingly along the smog blackened red-brick walls and run down into deep gutters to lurk in the darkness. Rats, so big and fat that you wonder how they got that way. If you were to go down into the sewers that run underground...your curiosity just might be answered.

I am afraid of rats, petrified of them. So scared in fact that if I was to see a rat face-to-face I know I would surely die. Natural scientists would have us all believe that no matter where we are, we are never more that three metres from a rat. The very thought makes my flesh crawl; I prefer to think that they live in dark and damp places and most of the time move around in silent packs. The only time you would hear them is when they are starving and scavenging for food so fiercely that they bite each other. That's when you will hear them squeal like the Devil.

Oh enough of this talk of rats and devils, I can hardly breathe, let us leave the filth and stench of their God-forsaken existence and go back up into the cool night air. Close your eyes again and drift along a dimly lit road and soon you will come to an alley that runs the whole length of the poverty stricken houses around it. Start at one end and you are sure to come full circle and return to the beginning. Whilst you float along that alley, make sure you open your eyes wide, for if you do not, you will not see that you are being followed by something of unspeakable evil.

There is no lighting in that alley. The only light is the ghostly blue of the winter moon hanging high in the midnight sky and casting eerie shadows behind you. Tune your eyes to the darkness, and do it quick before you take another step…you have been warned!

You know instinctively that you will need help before you reach the end of this alley…help to stay alive. *Will anyone hear your screams?* Halfway along that alley you will find a door, a door that is not locked but is almost impossible to open. Try as you might, you cannot turn the handle. You look back down the alley and there, coming ever closer is a crouching, grotesque shadow. *Is the moon playing tricks? Is it your shadow distorted by the debris scattered in the gutters of the alley? Please God let it be so!* Deep in your pounding heart you know that it is not your shadow; your lips tremble as you search for the forgotten words of the Lord's Prayer. The shadow creeps silently along the alley wall and your trembling turns to panic as it looms closer and closer. Your frantic fingers claw helplessly at the door handle and, as the shadow is almost upon you, your sad life ebbs away with every gushing sound of your own blood thrashing in your ears…your life is at an end. Your mouth forms into a silent scream, high-pitched and so unearthly that it splits the silence of the night, but the only ears your screams fall upon are those of the hunger crazed dogs that will feast on your flesh when the screaming stops…and those cursed rats!

You awaken, covered in great beads of sweat that run in rivers down your face and neck. You are sitting in your bed, eyes wide with fear and it takes several minutes for you to focus and realise you are in your own bed and safe at last from that terrifying beast. *Oh thank God it was just another nightmare… or was it?*

# Chapter One

The beautiful young woman of 24 years of age has all the wonders of the world waiting tantalizingly at her fingertips...or so it would appear if you took the scene before you at face value. She is acutely attuned to the sounds of movement around her, even in the darkness. You look at her refined bone-structure and delicate, flawless skin and nothing would make you believe, not even for one moment that her beauty belies a horror so gruesome that you will say that such a thing is not possible. Nothing could make you see that beneath that calm exterior is a fear so great that it would make the bravest of the brave tremble. Not the simple fears of something she does not know, but the impenetrable fears of the totally unknown. A calm voice, like the monotone tick-tock of a metronome hangs in the air about her ears and she is listening, listening only to the words *she* wants to hear. The rest are cast aside like a spoilt brat might toss away a birthday gift she was bored with. The owner of the voice believes that his hypnotic rhythm will have the desired effect but he is sadly mistaken, it is she who is hypnotising him and climbing into the darkest recesses of his mind. She laughs inwardly as the words seek out a reaction which she is not yet willing to give, after all, the game has hardly begun and she is enjoying her freedom. She waits until she hears that almost imperceptible lift in volume before she teases him with a muffled cry. The voice is trying to find the root of the nightmare she has had every third night for the past three years. Each time it lasts just a little bit longer, is a little scarier and always a little nearer the final climax.

Her name is Helena Albrecht and the voice is that of her psychiatric therapist.

The game she is playing is related to an invented nightmare. The nightmare began just after her 21$^{st}$ birthday and, at first, she put it down to just one incident and thought no more of it. Three nights later it happened again, but this time it lasted a little longer. It formed into a pattern, the same dream every third night, and each time a little more detail was revealed.

Helena was born on the 16<sup>th</sup> of March 1940 into a Germany that was at the height of its empire. Whilst other European countries succumbed one by one to the might of the German war machine Germany looked as though it would annex the world into the Third Reich. She was the only child of Joseph and Heidi Albrecht. They were both killed in an unexpected bombing raid on their hometown when Helena was barely six months old. The thought that the RAF would have the audacity to fly a bombing mission so deep into Germany would never have been imagined and although the air-raid sirens blasted out an early warning, most of the townsfolk thought it was nothing more sinister than an air-raid drill. The result of that complacency was that hardly anyone was in the air-raid shelter when the bombs began exploding in the direction of the railway yard which later appeared to have been the intended target. As in any raid like that it is inevitable that stray bombs would land on the homes of innocent civilians. Thankfully the tiny Helena was found by rescuers beneath the rubble of the house, covered and protected by her mother's dead body, they were amazed to find that amongst all that complete devastation was such a young child and without a scratch. News of her miraculous survival soon spread like wildfire round the town and it wasn't long before Helena's grandparents heard of the miracle but also learned the grim news of the death of their daughter. Helena was taken to hospital as a precaution but was released the following day into the protective arms of her Grandmother Yvette and her grandfather Hans.

And so it was that her life began with her maternal grandparents in a house not far from where her own parents had lived. Her grandparent's house had a little shell damage and a window had been blown in by the force of the detonation, but nothing major. Most of the other residents in the street had been lucky enough to have suffered no casualties.

The funeral of Helena's parents was a very sad affair, made all the more poignant by their age. The townsfolk were still reeling from the shock of the bombing raid but to learn that two young people as well loved as Joseph and Heidi had been killed in such a way was too much for them to bear. Old men cried openly as the horse drawn hearse moved slowly along the street carrying their coffins from the chapel to the cemetery, and women young and old clung to each other in desperate need of some kind of unspoken assurance that such a fate would not befall any more of their neighbours.

Most of the townsfolk worked for the railway which had been temporarily put out of action by the raid, so whilst it was being cleared they had time to give their lost loved ones a proper send off. At the graveside Yvette cradled Helena in her arms as her husband slid his arm around her shoulder. The coffins were placed side by side as the local priest blessed them with Holy Water and spoke quietly in Latin. A pair of doves broke from their roost in a nearby tree as the priest changed the volume of his voice to address the gathering. Yvette did not hear his words because she was deep in thought watching the birds as they winged their way skyward. *There you go my child, fly with your husband up to heaven where you belong.* She watched the birds until they disappeared from view then she slowly lowered her eyes to her beloved daughter's coffin. *Oh my baby, why did they take you from me like this? You never hurt a soul in all your life; you were such a good little girl. Why did the English take sides with those stinking French and those cowardly Poles? Did our forefathers not fight shoulder to shoulder against Napoleon at Waterloo? The Furher promised that the English would stand by us again to make the Aryan race the rightful masters of the world, even the English king is a German. What evil could make a nation as great as England turn its back on its own cousins and kill them like this?* Suddenly Yvette was brought out of her reverie by the deafening silence as all eyes turned to her. The priest was offering her the Holy water so that she may bless her daughter one last time. Before she took the water she looked down at the tiny bundle of life in her arms. She managed a weak smile at the priest and took the water, as she blessed the coffin she made the first of two vows. *Heidi, I will bring your daughter up to be a proud German, to love the fatherland and the Furher with all her heart.* As she sprinkled the water onto her son-in-law's coffin she made her

8

second vow. *I will avenge your death one hundred times over. The people who sent you both to Heaven I will send to Hell.*

As the coffins were slowly laid to rest, a mourner stepped forward to lay flowers by the graveside. Helena's grandfather put up his hand to stop them.

"No, do not lay your flowers here; my Daughter and her husband are not here. Come with us to the ruins of their house and lay your flowers there so that we can pray for their souls and pray for peace to come soon."

Yvette placed Helena in her grandfather's arms and together they walked in procession through the now deserted streets to what had been their daughter's house. Onto the black, charred ground where the house had stood Yvette led the mourners as they formed a circle almost as if it had been rehearsed a thousand times. It was so strange how some telepathic message of mutual unity and comfort seemed to permeate the air about them. Suddenly a young girl stepped forward and offered Yvette a single flower. Yvette stroked the girl's face and through the mist of her tears the face became that of her daughter. "Thank you my baby," she whispered as the young girl smiled and walked back to her weeping mother. Helena's grandfather stepped forward with Helena in his arms. "We will not rebuild this house," he said, "Instead we will build a garden of remembrance for my daughter and for all the children of Germany who have yet to sacrifice their lives for the freedom of the fatherland." He paused as he searched the faces of the mourners, "This was my only daughter and I am proud that she died for such a noble cause. There will be a time for sorrow and perhaps, when we have defeated our enemies, even a time for forgiveness, but for now, it is time to fight until our enemies are defeated and the lands stolen from us after the Great War are returned and the debts for their theft are paid for in full."

Yvette listened as her husband's words cut through the silence of the bleak day and her mind was ablaze with burning hatred. *There will be sorrow, there will be fighting, but there will never be a time for forgiveness. The English will pay their debt to me for the theft of my baby's sweet life.*

9

One by one the mourners moved to the centre of the circle to lay their wreaths, for them it was the end of a tragic story. In the darkest recesses of Yvette's mind the story was only just beginning.

# Chapter Two

The war in Europe raged on at lightning speed as the great German armies defeated one country after another and annexed them into the Third Reich that the Furher had promised would be the greatest empire the world had ever seen. The unstoppable Panza divisons brought Europe's capital cities into the sights of the blazing guns and the only possible outcome was surrender or annihilation...most of them thankfully chose to surrender.

Helena was brought up by her grandparents and of course by the spectre of the war. The community that had been built up during the world wide railway boom in the aftermath of the Napoleonic wars suddenly found a new sense of unity to bolster the one that had been so shaken by the loss of Helena's parents. So although Helena was brought up in such a potentially frightening era, she also felt the overwhelming security of a protective and staunchly patriotic community. As for her grandparents, well that was a very different story.

With the war going on all around her as she grew up, Helena often retreated alone into a world of magical fantasy. The stories of death and destruction that she gleaned from the whisperings of the town's adults were blocked out by the colour and beauty of a developing mind. Helena was a beautiful princess and lived in an enormous castle with servants to care for her every need. She would have gardens full of lovely flowers with birds and butterflies constantly around her. She would have lots of other children to play with and music would play all day long just for her. When the shadows fell and night came calling, instead of cowering beneath the course blankets of her blacked-out bedroom, she would sleep in a bed with silk sheets and huge fluffy pillows. She was happy in her dreams and... she was indestructible.

Not long after Helena's fifth birthday the news emerged that every German thought they would never hear. The Russians in the east were advancing towards Berlin and the allied forces in the west had broken through the last remaining defensive line leaving the whole of the Third Reich at the mercy of the victorious allies. It would only be a matter of time before the German High Command would have to surrender and the beloved Furher would be captured. Only five short years before, that outcome would have been unthinkable.

Helena's grandfather knew that it would only be a matter of days before allied tanks would be heard in the nearby countryside and after that, the tanks would be in the town square. He and the other town elders knew that they would either have to co-operate with the invading forces or fight them to the bitter end. Whichever fate awaited the men of the town they would have to make plans to save their young women from the obvious amorous advances of the victorious allied troops. They would have to find a way to protect them, so Hans called an emergency town meeting in the church.

He opened the meeting in the absence of the Bergermiester (the town Mayor) he had been called away to an emergency meeting of the Nazi party in the neighbouring town. He knew that the mayor had been summoned away to be briefed on arming the remaining men of the town to act as militia when the allied forces threatened their town. He also knew that their orders would be to fight to the death. Noble thoughts indeed and an ideal which many proud Germans would follow, but Hans was not only a patriot, he was a realist and he knew that it would serve no purpose at all to condemn the remaining men in the town to certain death and put the women at risk of retribution being taken out on them.

The townsfolk entered the hushed church hall and crowded in to the floor area below a low platform at the far end of the hall. On the platform was a single chair and desk which faced the floor, from his elevated position on the platform Hans could observe the sombre, forlorn faces of his neighbours as they filed in. Soon the room was filled almost to capacity yet still the sound of chatter did not rise much above a subdued whisper. There was a definite feeling of impending doom which hung heavily in the air like an executioner's axe about to fall and Hans knew that if he was to salvage anything at all for the future of his town he would need the strength of God in his voice and the courage and conviction of a latter day evangelist to deliver the speech of his life.

The room was suddenly shaken by the sound of Hans's voice and every ear turned to listen. "Some of you are my relatives, some of you are my friends, and all of you are my neighbours. Together we have laughed in good times, we have cried during bad times and we have all stood together in times of adversity. Never before has there been a need to stand together more than now. Not twenty miles from here our brave soldiers are fighting shoulder to shoulder against the relentless tide of the enemy invaders. As our children try to sleep in their beds at night they are wakened in fear by the sound of enemy guns. Soon those same guns will be raining shells on our village." One young rail worker stood staunchly to his feet, "And when those shells have done their bloody work and the foot soldiers follow in to take the town from us, we will rise from the ashes of our homes and we will fight for every inch of German soil, they will never take us alive!"
For the first time the gathering cheered and clapped as one supporting call echoed through the crowd after another. Hans was wise enough to allow them their moment of defiance before he called the meeting to order with nothing more than a wave of his giant hand. "My friend, your words are spoken like a true patriot; the Furher himself would be so proud of such a fine conviction, but perhaps there is another way."

"What other way can there be than to kill our enemies and drive them from our land?" Again the crowd cheered at his stirring battlecry. Hans slowly rose from behind his desk and walked purposefully to the front of the platform. "I believe you are right my friend, we should never allow ourselves to be enslaved or our great country to be occupied, but I have to ask you, how will our dead bodies and those of our children drive these invaders from our lands? There is a time for war and there is a time to sue for peace."

The man stood up again and asked in a bewildered voice: "Are you asking us to surrender?" Shouts of "Never!" reverberated round the hall as Hans once again took his time to answer. "No, I am asking you to use your heads instead of your hearts, I am asking you to give ourselves a real chance to become great again by planning a strategy for survival instead of planning a strategy for us to be wiped from the face of the earth. If our brave soldiers could not hold the English back on the beaches of Normandy after they had been dug into defensive positions for over five years, then how are we supposed to hold them back with nothing more than worn out hunting rifles and a few pitchforks?" Another man joined in the debate with a shout of: "How will I ever look my family in the face again if I do not do everything I can to fight our enemies?"

Hans nodded his head slowly: "That thought has crossed my mind too many times in the past few days, but the answer is in the question. If in the years to come you have to look your family in the face it will mean that you still have a family and they still have a father and that is why you chose not to fight."

The man could see the point that Hans made but he wanted more. "So are you saying that we should do nothing? There is not a man here who will stand by and do nothing"

The crowd once again erupted in cheers of support. Hans came back at him with the perfect answer. "I am not saying that we should do nothing, I am saying that we should fight on our terms. The Yugoslavians won their own freedom from us by fighting to their own strengths, by fighting in the hills which they controlled; let us learn a lesson from them. Right here we have something that the Allies want. We have a major railway station with lines spreading all over Germany. It is not a matter of if they take it; it is a matter of when they take it. If we appear to have had enough of this war and throw our hands up, they will ignore us in order to get on with the job in hand."

Everyone in the room was now intrigued at what exactly Hans was trying to propose, was it sabotage? Was it a guerrilla war that he was suggesting? "So what is the job in hand?" the man shouted, seemingly speaking on behalf of everyone else in the hall. Meanwhile Yvette was standing to the right of the platform and she was silently taking it all in and filtering through her own private thoughts. She was of course supporting her husband, but she was supporting him for very different reasons.

"Open your eyes and look beyond what is in front of your face. The Russian forces are weeks away from Berlin and the British and American armies are miles behind in the race. Both know that whichever army controls Berlin also controls the whole of the former German empire. In other words the whole future of Germany and with that control goes all the financial rewards. If we allow Berlin to fall completely into Russian hands we will never get it back. If the English and Americans win the race then we will have a chance to win it back, if not by force then by political means. So you see it is in our interests to let them take our town without a fight. There is also a way in which we can avoid immediate starvation. They will have to leave behind a garrison to protect the station and rail-yard and with a garrison comes food and supplies. They will need our labour to keep the railway running smoothly so we will in effect still be running the show. We can help ourselves to whatever we need and we can send it to where it is needed. We can fight them on our terms and as any good general will tell you, before you go to war you must build up your strength. We can use the rail-yard to do exactly that right under their noses."

It was with the talk of a garrison being nearby that Yvette's mind began to whirr with excitement, *with a garrison comes soldiers and the chance to avenge the death of my little girl.* Suddenly all eyes turned to Yvette as she began to speak in full support of her husband. "My husband is right, you all know that he fought bravely during the First World War and most of you stood with us in sorrow when we buried our beloved Heidi. Nobody wants to see these losses paid for in full more that Hans. To sacrifice our lives just to hold the enemy up for a few hours at the most would mean that we have given up hope. The German people are destined to rule the world and if that means that we have to start all over again then so be it. But to start all over again means that we first have to preserve what we have. We will not fight and neither will we run away from our enemies, we will not hide away our children or our women. We will stand together and stand tall as one community. We will take whatever they give us and in our silent endurance we will build our strength in body and in spirit until it is time to strike back at the heart of our enemies until they are gone from our land."

Everyone in the hall stood in silent amazement at the power of Yvette's irresistible delivery. Even Hans could hardly believe that the woman he had loved for over thirty years was capable of such a rousing oration. Hans looked out over the stunned faces in the hall and he knew that together he and his wife had convinced them that it was best to carry on with town life as if there had never been a war. He could never have known that his wife had very different reasons for wanting the allied soldiers to be so close at hand. One by one the townsfolk filed out of the hall and trudged back to their homes. Two weeks later British tanks rolled into the town and not one shot of resistance was fired, the townsfolk simply stayed at home. The first part of Hans's plan fell neatly into place as the army took control of the railway station and goods yard and called on all rail workers to report for work as usual and in return they would be fed. The first part of Yvette's plan also fell neatly into place when she saw the British engineers building sleeping quarters on the outskirts of the town for the soldiers who were about to garrison the town…they were right where she wanted them.

# Chapter Three

Sometimes, when Helena came home from school, grandfather Hans would be there. When she was six years old grandfather sat her on his knee and told her stories about his work. She would ask questions about the war and grandfather would answer every one of them as well as he could. She came home from school one day and grandfather was there to greet her. Helena liked it best when grandfather was home because grandmother was kinder to her when he was around. After tea, as usual, she sat on grandfather's knee under the ever watchful eye of grandmother. Helena took the chance and asked her grandfather about her parents. Grandfather Hans looked at his wife who simply nodded her head. Grandfather took a deep breath and began.

Heidi, their daughter, had been an only child. After she was born, grandmother had been unable to conceive any other children so all their love had been devoted to Heidi. She had met and married Gunther when she was 20 years of age. When she was 25 she discovered she was about to be a parent herself and Hans and Yvette had been delighted when she told them they were going to be grandparents. They had a comfortable, if not rich home in the middle of a bustling town and this was among the first places to be bombed during a raid by the allied forces. Her parents had both been killed protecting her from the rubble falling all around them. It was when her grandfather stopped speaking that Helena looked up and found tears running down her grandfather's face. She took her handkerchief from her pocket and carefully wiped the tears from his eyes then kissed him on the cheek. He looked at her and she offered a weak smile and grandfather gave her a squeeze in return showing he understood.

It was a rare occasion that Helena went to bed a happy child but she did that night. She had just slipped into bed and began to read her only book when her grandmother came into her room. She looked up from her book as her grandmother stood at the foot of the bed and said to her in a cold voice, "You are the child of my daughter, but you will never be as good as her. It was to save your life that she died, for that I will never forgive you." Helena watched in stunned silence as she turned around and walked out of the door closing it quietly behind her. Helena put down her book and thought of what her grandmother had just said. Now she began to vaguely understand why her grandmother did not like spending time with her and in her child's mind she began to piece together the knowledge that grandmother blamed her for the loss of her beloved daughter. She tried to work things through but things didn't make any sense. It was not her fault that her parents had died but if the grandmother needed someone to blame, why not blame the allies for dropping their bombs. There were many thousands killed in those raids, children were left without parents and some parents were left without children, but that was not her fault.

Two years passed and shortly after her eighth birthday, Helena's grandfather came into her room and sat on the end of her bed. He spoke to her as if she were an adult and tried his best to explain why grandmother was the way she was. Helena listened to all her grandfather said then said to him, "Grandfather, I know all you say is true, but why does grandmother blame me? I did not bomb the house or kill my parents. Is it just because I lived? Why does grandmother not realize that I too have a lot of pain? At least you had my mother for a lot of years, but I did not get the chance to know either of my parents." This was the most that Helena had spoken in all her eight years. She had kept all her feelings locked up inside of her, not once daring to say what was etched onto her young heart. The words were spoken with such great emotion that Helena could not stop crying, she hated herself for it because she was determined to be strong. Grandfather put his arm around her shoulders and held her close to him. She cried and cried until at last she could cry no more and fell asleep wrapped in her grandfather's arms.

Grandfather gently laid Helena on her bed and covered her with a blanket, stroked her face and left her sleeping. Only when he stood up and turned toward the door, did he see grandmother standing in the doorway. She had heard every word Helena had said. The look she gave Helena told grandfather everything he needed to know. Here stood a woman he did not recognise, she was wrapped up in her own emotions, there were no feelings but hatred for the child sleeping in front of her. Grandfather looked at grandmother and said in a quiet voice, "She is our grandchild. Try to show her a little compassion."

"No, I will not. She should have died with her parents. As long as I live, she will receive no love from me," was her barbed reply. Grandfather shook his head and said in a dejected tone: "Then I shall have to love her for both of us. She is our flesh and blood. Someone has to care for her, as you heard for yourself, she is hurting too. Can't you see that our daughter would have wanted us to love her like she did. If you can't bring yourself to love her then Heidi will have died for nothing."

"Our daughter died, protecting her, we had a perfect life until she came along, she took everything from me; she is the devil!"

Hans walked over to the old fireplace and taking a thin piece of wood he held it into the flames to light his pipe. There was no point in trying to reason with her when she was in one of her depressions. Yvette stood watching the retreat of her husband for quite some time and it made her sick. *Go on, protect that bitch, do the devils bidding, but I warn you, I will have my revenge.* Looking first at him and then at the little girl sleeping in her bed. She walked into the room and stood at the foot of Helena's bed to watch her sleeping. Although she could still see the pain written on her granddaughter's face and could still recall every word she had said, the look on her face said she did not care what happened to the child. To Yvette, her granddaughter's life was meaningless…but it would not always be so.

19

## Chapter Four

In each of our lives, there are times that we can look back and say 'They were great times' and for most of us those times are back in our childhood years. Even in old age when our memories fade, somehow the birthdays and Christmas Eves that were so magical are indelibly branded on our inner beings. Sadly this was not the case for the young Helena. At the age of eight, there should have been so many happy times; looking back it should have been impossible to decide which times were better than others. Yet for Helena, happy times were few and far between, so when a happy time came along, she grabbed at it with both hands. In just a few weeks, she would be nine years of age, but for her there would be no birthday party to forge a lasting joy in her memory. Grandmother would never allow such an extravagance, let alone have other children in the house. Helena sensed by now, that her grandmother had no love for her, but she knew equally by the little things that he did that her grandfather had more than enough love to make up for it. Now that the war was long over, Helena would come home from school to see grandfather waiting at the door for her. There would always be a smile on his face and his strong arms were open wide waiting to give her a huge hug. Every night she would sit with grandfather and tell him of her day at school, and he would help her with her homework. Grandmother would sit in her chair knitting, never speaking, never smiling, she just stared stoically at the fire in the hearth with perhaps a sideways glance every once in a while at Helena. The child was not really aware of her grandmother's strange behaviour, over the years she had grown used to it. She did however sense with the optimism of a child that one day she would soon have a reason to smile again.

Another two months went by and Helena reached her ninth birthday. Each year she had dreamed of the same kind of wonderful surprises that she heard her school friends talk of and each year she was to be so cruelly disappointed, but not this year...this year was special! Quite out of the blue her grandfather asked if she would like a party to which she could invite her school friends. At first Helena was confused, how could she have a party when her friends would never be allowed into the house? Her grandfather had the answer. "Your dear mother had such a wonderful ninth birthday party; it was filled with magic and happiness. We bought her a pony and to this very day I can see how the sight of it made her face light up. Your mother was beautiful, but when she smiled there was no beauty on Earth to compare." Helena was so thrilled because it meant that for the very first time she could have a birthday just like all her friends. Now that food was not so scarce and rationing was not as frequent, it was with a happy heart that Helena went shopping with her grandfather. They planned to buy bread for sandwiches and cup-cakes and fresh lemonade and they took great delight in talking about spending the whole day preparing the delicacies for Helena and her friends.

The day of the party arrived and Helena was up and dressed early to help grandfather. He made sure that her day was indeed going to be special. He re-lived all the things he and Helena's mother had done all those years before. They laughed and joked and had a fabulous day. By tea-time, all her friends had arrived and each guest seemed more laden with gifts than the previous one. Most of her friends were the children of the occupying armed forces personnel from Britain and the United States, so the gifts they could afford looked as if they were from a different world. Helena had never had a day like it, she couldn't have known it at the time, but she would never have a day like it again. Her grandmother had remained locked in her room in a self-imposed exclusion while all the festivities were going on. Hans had pleaded with her, for the sake of the child right up until the first guest arrived, but it was not to be and as the party unfolded in the rooms below her feet she cursed each sound of laughter as if it were a sting from a demented scorpion trapped in a ring of fire.

Later in the evening, parents had begun to arrive to take their children home again and by eight the last ones had gone and the house was bereft of laughter once more. Only then did grandmother venture downstairs to stoically tell Helena it was time for bed. Even grandmother's coldness towards Helena could not stop her from smiling on that most special of days.

After saying goodnight to grandfather, Helena climbed the stairs to her room; she closed the door and got into bed with the smiling faces of her friends on her mind and the sounds of their laughter still ringing in her ears. In the darkness she reflected on how good and happy the day had been; the excitement still so close to the surface of her heart would not allow her to sleep. It was well into the night before she finally fell into a happy dream filled sleep. She dreamt of rainbows and giant flowers in a magical garden in an exotic land far, far away. Birds swooped and called in wondrous song as they flitted amongst the trees and in the centre of the garden she saw her mother's pony. It was surrounded by all the children who had come to enjoy her party. Later, she would walk through the garden where she came across a maze. Walking through this maze, she eventually arrived at the centre to find her grandmother sitting on a stool. Helena stepped back startled. That was the last place she expected to find her grandmother, she belonged to a place without love and a land without colour. She looked again but found that her grandmother was smiling back at her. She beckoned her closer, "Do not be afraid," she whispered, "We have games to play and I have so many stories to tell you, I have wasted so much time blaming you for something you were not guilty of."

Helena's beautiful dream was shattered when the morning came by the sounds of shouting downstairs. She crept silently out of bed and quietly opened her door. The sounds of raised voices covered the creaking of the floorboards beneath her feet and she was able to sit on the landing to listen. The muffled shouts that woke her could clearly be heard and she realised that her grandmother was shouting at grandfather. She could hardly believe her ears when her grandmother hissed that she wanted Helena out of *her* house. She gave him an ultimatum, either Helena left or she would, she could not stand to live under the same roof for one more night. Eventually the shouting subsided and Helena felt that it was safe to go downstairs; her plan was to pretend that she had only just woken. At the foot of the stairs Helena looked down the full length of the hallway and saw her grandfather sitting at the kitchen table, and even though he smiled weakly she could clearly see the tears of frustration on his lined face. She walked tentatively into the kitchen half hoping that the argument she heard had been part of her dream. The look of anger on her grandmother's face as she walked past her told her that her hopes were in vain. When he was certain that his wife was out of earshot he whispered, "Did you hear any of what your grandmother said?" Helena simply nodded. "She did not mean these wicked things my child," he said. "You have to find it in your heart to understand that you remind her so much of your mother and that is why she says these things."

Helena took her grandfather's hand, "I always try to be a good girl to make grandmother happy but I know she does not want me here and I have known it for a long time. I thought I could make her love me. When I am old enough I will find another place to live."

Her grandfather patted her hand, "You are so grown up, just like your beautiful mother; you know that I will always love you."

Helena went back to her bedroom and sat on the edge of her bed. As she ran the jumble of her grandmother's words of hatred and her grandfather's words of love over and over again in her mind to try to make sense of it all she suddenly felt so dreadfully alone. The wonderful birthday party she had only the day before lay in the ruins of her troubled mind. It was too much for any child to bear and her young shoulders slumped as her heart broke into a thousand pieces. The reality of knowing for certain that being loved by her grandmother was never going to happen left her crushed in a world of desolation.

The next day Helena resolved to hatch a plan, but first she had to buy herself some time and to do that she knew she had to stay well away from her grandmother. She knew that her grandfather would do everything he could to keep her safe until she was old enough to leave but she could also see that he was beginning to look increasingly frail. Helena learned very quickly how to be cunning and deceitful, she developed an almost sixth sense that was incredibly accurate; it was tuned to alert her when grandmother was about to come home or enter a room and she heeded its warning with lightning speed. It was almost as if she had learned how to vanish into thin air at will. She kept up this game of cat-and-mouse for several weeks until one day her grandmother caught her completely off guard. Helena was in the garden—a place where she felt safe and secure—she often went out in the early evening to gaze up at the twilight stars and imagine that the brightest stars in the sky were the souls of her mother and father. *Oh mother can't you make grandmother love me so that we can live a normal life? If that is you shining down on me tonight please take the hatred away from grandmother's heart and let her love again like she loved you.* Helena was too pre-occupied wishing on a star to notice that she was not alone. Suddenly she felt an icy hand reach into her body and clamp its ghostly, frozen grip around her heart. She turned to find herself face-to-face with her grandmother. She fully expected her to raise her hand and bring it down hard onto her face, but she had never been so mistaken. Instead of lashing out her grandmother smiled and said: "Helena, would you stay and sit with me a while?"

Helena did not know what to say and even if she did she knew the words would not form in her mouth. Her grandmother continued without an answer. "It has been several weeks since we last spoke and I have had time to reflect on the way I have treated you."

Helena stole a glimpse at the glistening star above her grandmother's head and thought, *Have you answered my prayers moma?*

"I feel that perhaps the time is right to put the past behind us, don't you agree?" Her grandmother said. Helena had to think fast, her sixth sense was screaming at her turn and run but instead she stood her ground. "Does this mean that you want me to stay after all Grandmother?" Helena asked.

Her grandmother's faced darkened, "Little girls should not listen in to conversations that do not concern them."

"If I am to leave this house then does that not concern me?"

"You are too clever for your own good," her grandmother snapped when she realised that Helena knew more than she thought.

"I heard you shouting at grandfather that if I didn't leave then you would. Why do you hate me so much? Why are you pretending to change your mind? No, you don't love me. You don't even want me here so I don't want to sit and talk to you," Helena said as she walked from the garden and into the house leaving her grandmother alone with her bitterness.

Helena wasn't certain if it was her stand against her grandmother that perhaps made her think again, but whatever it was, the question of her leaving the house was never brought up again until the following year. Since her birthday party Helena had become increasingly popular with a wider circle of friends, she was no longer thought of as the 'odd' girl who spent most of her time alone.

One day at the end of the school day she said goodbye to her friends and began the walk home where she knew grandfather would be waiting at the door for her. When she arrived at the house, her grandparents were not at home. She looked under the plant pot outside the back door and found the spare key. She let herself in and began to call for her grandfather but there was no answer. She looked all round the house and in the garden but neither was anywhere to be seen. She went back into the house and stood in the middle of the parlour wondering where they could possibly be. She wasn't bothered about her grandmother but it was so unlike her grandfather not to be there when she arrived home from school. She had just decided to go to her room when she heard the front door being opened and her grandparents raised voices. They went straight through the hallway and into the kitchen, Helena stayed in the parlour doorway listening as the topic unfolded. Above her grandfather's quiet voice, she could hear her grandmother shouting: "I don't care if her friends want to come and play with her, I am sick of that little bitch twisting you around her little finger. I have not forgotten last year when I had to listen to the laughter of the children of our own beloved daughter's murderers, right here in the house she grew up in!"

"Yvette, how can you call them murderers, we were at war for God's sake!"

"Our baby never declared war on anyone, she wouldn't hurt a fly and they murdered her just as if they had strangled her right in front of our eyes. I will never forgive them and neither should you. I will not rest until every last one of them is driven from our land. I don't want that girl in this house, she is more English than German,"

"She doesn't speak a word of English, how can you say that?" he asked incredulously.

"If you lay down with pigs, you become a pig whether you sound like one or not. She spends all her time with them so she has become one of them. I want her out of my home and out of the home of her mother's sweet childhood. She must go to the orphanage. If you won't take her, then I will."

Hans looked at her with pleading eyes, "She is our grand-daughter. We have a responsibility to care for her my love. She is our flesh and blood; we can not cast her into the care of strangers,"

Neither one of the grandparents had noticed that Helena was standing in the doorway listening to every stinging word. Helena managed to creep up to her room in the height of their argument; she didn't want either of them to know that she could hear every word. That night she wondered how she could make things easier for her grandfather and decided to run away. Robotically she packed a few things into her school bag and waited. Several hours passed until eventually she heard her grandparents come up the stairs and go to bed. This night grandfather went into the spare room to sleep. He was so angry with his wife that he turned his back on her and shut the door. Helena waited for another cold hour to make sure they were asleep then she quietly opened her bedroom window, climbed out onto the ledge, down the drainpipe and, without looking back, walked away from all that anger and hatred.

# Chapter Five

Morning came and grandfather went to get Helena up for school. He opened her door and immediately saw that her bed had not been slept in and the window was wide open. He looked out of the window up and down the street, but of course Helena was nowhere to be seen. Going to the grandmother's room, he shouted at her, "Get up Yvette Helena's not in her room, we have to find her." His wife did not move. Instead she simply pulled the blanket up under her chin and said: "Good, it will save me taking her to the orphanage today", then she turned over to go back to sleep. Hans was furious, he clawed at the blankets like a madman dragging them off the bed which made his wife sit up and glare at him. Never before had she seen him so angry. The look on his face told her she had better do as he said. Reluctantly, she got out of bed, washed and dressed quickly and went downstairs where he was waiting for her.

She stopped at the kitchen door and looked at her husband. He was sitting at the kitchen table frantically wringing his hands and she could see he was wondering where Helena could have gone. The pain and anger in his face spoke volumes to her. Never before had she seen him so affected, even when their daughter was killed, he did not respond like this. She felt embarrassed at her initial reaction to him finding Helena's bedroom empty and in her way she felt a strange, sickly kind of pity for him. She walked into the kitchen and tried to put her hands on his shoulders, but he shrugged her off and left the kitchen. Yvette realised that her hatred for Helena had pushed him too far. She knew the only way to regain her position of dominance over him was to look as if she was prepared to help find Helena. She had put on her hat and coat as Hans was already leaving the house to begin the search. He carried with him Helena's coat. It had been such a cold night and it was obvious that Helena had not taken her coat with her; to do so she would have had to creep through the house and risk waking them; he knew that if and when he found her she was bound to be freezing, perhaps even frozen to death.

Helena had walked all night and eventually found herself walking along a deserted railway line. She found a shed without a lock and she tentatively wandered inside to shelter from the freezing conditions. Several small panes of glass were missing from the windows and there were a few holes in the roof, but at least it offered some shelter from the cold night air. She looked around her and found on the floor of the shed, among the dust and spiders, some old newspapers. Using some of the papers as a pillow, she covered herself with the rest and curled up to try to sleep. Eventually she drifted off into a shallow, restless sleep. She woke the next morning, cold, confused and terribly hungry. She couldn't take any food from the house for the same reason that she had left without her coat. She realised that perhaps she should have planned things through properly before she left. She needed money to buy food and if she was not in a position to earn it, the only thing left to do was steal it or go back home.

From the relative sanctuary of the shed she began to work on a possible plan. She thought of going to school where at least she would be warm and at lunchtime there would be a hot meal for her. She quickly dismissed that thought when she realised that was the first place her grandparents were likely to look and after not finding her they would question her friends which in-turn would make begging food from them impossible, they would either talk her in to going home or they would betray her. It was not in Helena's nature to steal, but it was rapidly becoming her only option. If she stayed where she was it would just be a matter of time before she froze to death, so she decided to keep moving. She walked along the railway track until she came to a path leading up to the road. It was a road she didn't recognise so in a way that was a good sign, it meant that she was moving in the right direction…away from home. Walking along the road she kept her eyes open for opportunities to find food. Perhaps there would be food in the rubbish bins behind any shops that might come into view where old food had been discarded. The shops would not be open yet, she sensed it was too early but the bins outside would probably still have left over food from the previous day.

She had been on the road without seeing anyone else, it was deserted, then, something happened which made her heart sink further still, it began to snow and it looked like the early morning sky was full. The wind began to swirl the heavy snowflakes all around her and she knew she was in trouble. She had seen the signs before as grandfather had taught her how to read the sky. She had to find food and shelter soon because there was a blizzard on the way. She pulled her poor cardigan up around her neck and headed into the wind. The snow began to fall more heavily and her fingers froze as she held her cardigan as tight as she could. She looked into the distance as the snow stung her eyes and for a moment it looked as though the outline of a building came into view. She couldn't be certain because the wind was blinding her. All she could do was hope and pray that what she had seen was not a mirage. On and on she struggled and sure enough she could clearly see a building up ahead. There was a sign by the side of the road with the name of the town on it but the name was obscured by the snow, her fingers were too cold to wipe the snow away to see where she was and besides to do so would waste precious time. She reached the house only to find that it was a disused signal box. It didn't matter though; the signs were still good, not much further along she could see other houses and where there were houses there would be shops. She turned down the first street she came to and immediately collided with a snow covered figure in front of her. She had just begun to apologise and ask for help when she looked up and found herself staring into the face of… her grandfather! In her confused state of hunger and cold she had turned back towards the town as she left the deserted railway hut she had sheltered in the night before. All the time she thought she was moving further away from home she was in fact moving back towards it.

"Oh my baby I am so glad to have found you," her grandfather wept as he bent to wrap her coat around her and she put her arms around him, hugging him so tightly. "I'm sorry for running away grandfather, but I know that grandmother does not want me in the house anymore. I thought it would be better for you if I wasn't there."

"Oh Helena, you are so wrong. Your grandmother is not well, she doesn't know what she is saying; you have to understand that. We will take her to see a doctor and soon things will all be as they should be. The main thing is that you are back with me and you are safe and well." With that he gathered her up in his strong arms and carried her home.

Grandmother was sitting in the parlour staring blankly into the flames of the fire. When she heard the door opening she expected her husband to walk in alone. She was surprised when she saw Helena as her grandfather gently put her down on the floor. Looking at his wife he said, "Get her some hot food. She is hungry, cold and tired." Without any sign of emotion and not daring to answer him, she turned in silence to do as she was told. Hans stood and watched as she walked into the kitchen then, putting his arm around Helena's shoulders, led her into the parlour to sit in the armchair beside the warmth of a roaring fire. In complete exhaustion she fell asleep watching the flames dancing in the grate. Grandfather let her sleep until her food was ready.

He watched as her shaking hands took hold of the spoon and she began to eat. When he was sure that there would be no long lasting effects of her ordeal out in the snow he carried her to bed, where she slept soundly until the next morning.

In the days and weeks that followed, the episode was forgotten and in the months after that the house seemed to have lost its underlying feeling of tension and anger. Grandfather had given Yvette an ultimatum; that she either left Helena alone or he would have her committed to a mental hospital. Yvette was a bitter woman with a twisted, vengeful view of the world but she was no fool. She would melt back into life on his terms and she would bite her tongue until the time was ripe for her to take control.

Spring came and the early flowers began to bloom, the birds returned from warmer climes and the trees were once again covered in foliage. Grandmother had been nicer to Helena since the day she had run away and Helena was happier than she had ever been. She had begun to notice changes in herself as well. She was looking forward to going to high school with her friends—whom she was allowed to see more of—and together they would chatter excitedly about the prospects ahead of them. Germany had suffered terribly in the latter stages of the war and most of its once proud cites were left in ruins, but gradually a new Germany was rising from the ashes of the devastation and nowhere was this more evident than in the education system. The new German administration knew that Germany could only truly rise again through the education of its young people. Other things in her life changed too. Gone were the days when she needed someone to look after her. She had begun to do more things for herself, like cook her own food if her grandparents were not at home and iron her own clothes. She was growing into a very independent young lady and both her grandparents had also noticed the changes in her physical appearance. These weren't the only changes taking place; there were changes in both her grandparents. Not long after Helena's failed runaway attempt she noticed that grandfather had moved his things into the spare bedroom. She knew that they seldom spoke where once they chatted endlessly. Apart from the odd occasion when they happened to be in the house at the same time there was no contact at all between them anymore. Helena would have had to be blind not to have noticed these changes and one day asked her grandfather if he still loved her grandmother, his reply was strange and ambiguous, "As long as you are here I'll be fine." At first Helena took that to mean that he was still unsure if she would run away again, but the wonderful changes in her life had chased those thoughts from her head forever. "Don't worry grandfather, I won't run away again," she smiled as she reached over to gently stroke his hand. She had no way of knowing it then but before that night was over she would have very different thoughts.

It began innocently enough with grandfather sitting on the edge of the bed talking to Helena as if she were an adult, which in many ways she was. Slowly grandfather eased his way further onto the bed. Helena was not unduly worried by this in fact she was pleased because she missed his goodnight cuddles. She snuggled her head against his chest as he moved to sit beside her with his back resting on the wall behind the bed. Slowly he put his arm around her shoulders. She felt his hand pushing in her back as if she was being guided onto his body and she resisted, she tried to move away thinking at first that he had fallen asleep but her heart turned cold when she realised that he was forcing her hand to touch him. She became frightened and tried hard to push him away but he was too strong for her. Suddenly a myriad of fragmented thoughts flooded into her brain. She knew she was too small to stop him doing anything he wanted so she couldn't fight. She couldn't call her grandmother for help either because that would only fall on deaf ears. Something screamed at her to bite and scream, but another voice more powerful and convincing whispered into her soul that her life would be so beautiful from then on if she just relaxed and enjoyed what was happening. What she didn't realise through all the confusion was that it was the voice of her grandfather. She allowed her hand to be guided to his intimate parts as he pushed his free hand between her legs. She closed her eyes and lay motionless on the bed as he pushed up her nightdress and ripped her underwear from her. The rest of her ordeal was forced to the darkest recesses of her mind. Her maidenhood had been brutally stolen from her by the only man she had ever known and that night was to be the first of many.

# Chapter Six

Helena Maria Schultz stands at 5'6" in height, has dark brown eyes and long chestnut brown hair. With a fair complexion, red full lips and a very good figure, Helena was regarded as a beautiful woman by all who met her. She lies on the psychiatrist's couch and is hypnotised to regress into her past.

As a defence against the terrible attacks by her grandfather that she had endured for so long and kept hidden from the world, she would indulge in secret fantasies where she would leave her hometown to study at the newly re-built University of Berlin. She dreamt of one day becoming a doctor or a lawyer so she studied hard at school and learned every lesson well. To all who knew her she was the epitome of a studious, focused German girl responding to the challenges of rebirth and regeneration of the Fatherland. However, in secret and away from the eyes of the world Helena was learning other things of a darker nature which she would soon unleash onto an unsuspecting Germany.

Besides being her torturer, her grandfather was also her keeper and her will to survive made it possible to slip into a different world whenever he called to commit his evil deeds. She resolved to endure her intrusions on her body until she was old enough to do something about it herself. The imaginations of how that day would end were enough to drive her on with the determination of a starving lioness.

On her way home from school one day, she passed an alleyway which seemed to run full circle. She went down the alleyway and walked the full length of it only to find that she was back at the beginning. *How very strange,* she thought. Halfway along the alley, she noticed a box and on closer inspection she heard a faint and pitiful cry from within. She opened it, and found a kitten inside that was not more than a few days old. It had obviously been left to die so Helena tucked it under her coat and took it home with her. She knew that she had a lot of love to give but no-one to share it with. She also had a terrible secret that was too disgusting to ever speak of to any other human being. In that poor kitten she had found the perfect soulmate and the perfect confessor.

Every day after school Helena would hurry home to be greeted by Benjamin and over the following years the two became inseparable. Her grandfather's attacks continued all through her puberty and she withstood them with a deepening stoicism. Sometimes the attacks would stop for a while but she knew that they would resume at some point. The only way they would ever stop was when she put a stop to them, and the plans to do just that were well under way.

## Chapter Seven

The 5<sup>th</sup> of November 1954 was to be a date that would change Helena's life forever, but only four days before that date her life looked set to carry on in torment until the day she died. The first day of November arrived just like any other day, it was a Monday morning and Helena was up and dressed ready to go to school when something quite unusual happened. She noticed at the breakfast table that both her grandfather and grandmother were dressed in their formal clothes used only on special days. She wasn't told exactly why that was but during breakfast her grandfather casually announced that they may not be home when she came home from school because they had business to attend to in the city. Helena didn't even bother to guess what the business might be because she already knew that if it was serious enough to warrant grandmother going into the city then it could only be something they could immediately profit from—probably the death of a relative who had left them some money. "It may be after nine o'clock this evening when we are home so put yourself to bed when you have eaten something," her grandfather said. Helena left for school, and walked as if she was on air with a feeling of freedom.

The day couldn't pass quickly enough so that she could hurry back to the house. She had always wanted to see the photographs of her mother and father that she knew her grandmother kept hidden away from her. Now she had the perfect opportunity to finally look upon the faces of her parents. She had to be careful with any drawers or cupboards she opened because her grandmother would know if anything was left out of place. Helena dashed out of the school gates the moment the bell rang and within ten minutes she was standing in her grandmother's bedroom looking fixedly at the chest of drawers in front of her. Her hands were shaking as she tentatively ran her fingertips over the handles. If she pulled the drawer open there would be no looking back. She closed her eyes and pulled the first drawer wide open. Her heart sank when instead of seeing photo albums filled with smiling pictures of her mother and father she saw nothing but a drawer crammed full of her grandmother's smalls. One after the other Helena opened the remaining drawers and each one led to further disappointment. It soon became obvious that if she was to find anything at all she would have to look in more secretive places; the problem was where? There would be nothing in her grandfather's room, of that she was fairly certain. She went out onto the landing and it was then that her eyes were drawn to the wooden hatch in the ceiling that blocked the entrance to the attic. *Of course, that's where she must keep them!*

Helena looked at the clock and saw that she had less than two hours to find a way into the attic, find what she was looking for and put everything back in exactly the same place as she had found them. She remembered the step ladder down in the garden shed so she made her way downstairs and unlocked the back door. After making sure the coast was clear from the prying eyes of her neighbours Helena quickly unlocked the garden shed and carried the ladders into the house. Within minutes she was lifting the heavy hatch and peering into the pitch black darkness of the attic. Once the hatch was fully open she could see a candle and a box of matches just within arms length of the opening. She reached in and lit the candle before she climbed into the attic. She found herself standing in a room that she had never been in before surrounded by boxes of all shapes and sizes. She looked for a box which looked as if it might contain a photo album, it would of course be rectangular and relatively flat. She peered into the shadowy corners of the attic made eerie by the flickering of the candle flame. There it was in the darkest recess of the attic, a flat box with the forbidden treasure! She walked over to the box and lifted it onto another box which brought it up to just above her waist. The box was heavier than she thought it should be, but then again the cover could be inlaid with heavy pattern work of leather or wood. She held her breath as she lifted the lid and saw before her eyes…an army issue Luger 9mm semi automatic pistol, the box also contained three 8 round flat magazines. Helena closed the lid and began to cry, she had been looking for life—the lost life of her parents—and once again she had found death, or the means to take life. She realised that she was crying for her lost childhood and for all the happy times she should have had. The thought of taking hold of the pistol and ending her young life had passed through her mind on several occasions before that fateful day when she had prayed that she too could have perished with her parents.

This was not the kind of life a child should have, in fact this was not a life at all, but simply an existence in a world of hatred, no love, and abuse by the people who should have loved her. Slowly she opened the lid again and took hold of the Luger, *How easy it would be for me to take my life. One small pull of the trigger and life would be snuffed out in less than a second.*

Helena put the Luger on the floor beside her and carefully replaced the box in exactly the same place she had found it. She spent the following hour making certain that there was no trace of what she had been up to. By the time her grandparents came home at nine o'clock Helena was in her bed with the light off…waiting for her grandfather to sit on her bed and begin his evil ritual.

That night Helena held her breath as her grandfather turned the handle of her bedroom door. Her fingers tightened round the handle of the luger. She knew that she had to wait until he was close enough for her not to miss. The door opened and her grandfather switched on the light…something he had not done before. "Are you sleeping my baby?" he asked. Her stomach turned at the sound of his voice but she managed to force an answer that would not give her true feelings away. "I have only been in bed for a few minutes grandfather because I had a lot of school work to do."

"Then you should sleep my baby, I don't want you to miss any of your school work, I want you to make your mother proud of you," he said. With that he turned out the light and closed the door leaving her to tremble in the darkness at the thought of what she had almost done. The only time since he began violating her she had prayed that he would come into her room and he didn't. *How cruel this life is.*

The fact that she couldn't use the gun that night left her with another dilemma. Where would she hide the gun whilst she was at school? She couldn't leave it under her pillow because her snooping grandmother was sure to find it. She sat up in her bed in the darkness and peered around the room. A thin slither of light from the rising moon shone through the gap in the curtains like a rapier and illuminated a length of the floor. That beam of light gave her an idea. She remembered watching her grandfather working in her room years ago and she had watched him lifting one of the floorboards to work on the wiring beneath it, all she had to do was find out which one it was. She tried to think back and remembered that he had moved the rug into the centre of the room to lift the floorboard, so that was a good place to start. Silently she pulled the rug to the far end of her bedroom and on all fours she began quietly tapping each board until she found one that sounded as if it was not secure. She knew she was taking a chance by tapping but she really had no other choice, they would surely find it if she didn't hide it and she had every intention of using it when the opportunity next presented itself. It wasn't long before she knew that her memory had served her well. One floorboard she tapped sounded hollow and she saw that it was half as long as the others. She picked at the end of the floorboard with her fingernails until it eased up just enough for her to put her hand underneath to lift it fully out. The space beneath it was perfect; she lowered the gun into the cavity and gently lowered the floorboard back into place. She pulled back the rug and went back to bed not knowing that on the following morning she would be presented with the perfect opportunity to make the torture stop from a most unlikely source.

The next morning, Helena went down to breakfast knowing that she had to act as she always did. In her young mind she imagined that she may perhaps be carrying her thoughts around for the world to see and the slightest deviation from her normal routine would make them think that she was up to something. That thought was of course nonsense but that is how guilt manifests itself in the minds of people who are fundamentally innocent yet forced into thinking like a criminal. A criminal has no conscience, they are detached from emotion. *How cruel this life is.*

The first test was passed without incident, both grandparents sat silently at the table and neither paid much attention to their granddaughter. They didn't see her shaking hands and they didn't hear that her heart was beating so fast that it was about to explode. She slipped from the table and left for school with a simple 'Goodbye' from her grandfather; grandmother, as usual, behaved as if she didn't exist.

Helena had only been in the school grounds for little more than a minute when two of her best friends appeared and began to chat to her excitedly about the bonfire their parents had planned for them for the Friday evening. Helena had no idea what a bonfire party was until her friends explained that it was a British tradition to burn an effigy of Guy Fawkes and let off fireworks and bangers. She turned down their invitation to visit the British forces base, but not before making a mental note that Friday night was going to be alive…with loud bangs that no one would pay any attention to. It was then that she hatched her plan for freedom.

That evening as Helena arrived home from school, she found her grandfather waiting for her. "I missed you yesterday," he whispered softly so that Yvette could not hear. Helena knew that remark and his manufactured expression of affection—which would appear genuine to an outside observer—meant that he would probably pay her a visit later that night to satisfy his evil lust and her heart sank. Still, she had a few hours before bedtime so that would give her time to think. In her bedroom she looked at the carpet at the spot beneath where the gun was hidden, *I can't do it tonight because everyone in the town would hear the gun, I must wait until Friday, until then I must let him do what he will.* Having that thought gave her the basis for her plan.

Later that night as she lay in bed she heard him leave his room and her body stiffened uncontrollably as it always did. Moments later he was at the bedroom door, he turned the handle and made his way through the darkness to her bed. Without saying a word he lifted the bed sheets and climbed into her bed. He did the same as he always did as Helena waited for the muffled groan that indicated he was finished and her ordeal would be over for another night. As he got out of bed he was surprised to hear Helena speak. "Grandfather, some friends from school have told me that there will be fireworks on Friday night over at the British forces barracks..." Her grandfather cut her short, "I don't want you to go anywhere near your friends out of school, you know the trouble it will cause with your grandmother."

Helena reached out and touched his hand, "What I was going to say grandfather is that I don't like fireworks and I wanted to know if you would come and sit with me until it is over."

Her grandfather took her hand and held it to his lips, "Why of course I will my darling."

As he left the room Helena almost wretched with a mixture of disgust and the nerves knotting up her stomach. She had prayed that she could find the strength to bring herself to talk to him after what he had just done. Despite her feeling of nausea she was relieved, even happy that the first part of her trap had been laid.

The rest of the week seemed to crawl by so painfully slowly. Her invitation to her grandfather seemed to have had the effect that it stopped him from calling on her in the middle of the night for the rest of the week. Perhaps he was saving himself because in his sick mind he knew that he would get what he wanted on Friday night and that his company would be welcome.

Friday night finally came and at six o'clock just before the fireworks display started in earnest Helena made her way up to her room watched very closely by her grandfather. Her grandmother sat by the fireplace reading the evening newspaper seemingly in a world of her own. Helena couldn't tell how long it would be before her grandfather would make his move so she had to act quickly, there would be no room for mistakes. The moment her bedroom door closed behind her she almost threw herself to the floor. She dragged the carpet back and clawed at the floorboard, her heart was racing as the fireworks began to explode loudly in the evening sky all over the town. She lifted the gun from its hiding place and after replacing the carpet she sat on the bed in the darkened room. The minutes ticked by like hours as she stared fixedly at the door handle, suddenly the moment she had waited for arrived. Her grandfather turned the handle and quietly entered the room. He stood in the darkness with his back to Helena as he closed the door so that his wife would not hear it. "Do not be afraid my darling, you grandfather is here to protect you," he said as he walked towards the bed. Helena's eyes had long since become accustomed to the failing light and she levelled the gun at his head with her finger on the trigger. Her hand began to tremble violently, *Wait until you can not miss,* the voice in her head commanded. As he lowered his upper body to sit on the bed Helena squeezed the trigger and his head snapped backwards as the bullet hit him in the throat. The sound of the blast blended in perfectly with the noise of the fireworks and as a bright red glow illuminated the sky and permeated the room she looked down at her grandfather's bulging eyes as his mouth made a horrible gurgling sound. She calmly sat on the bed and watched as his life slipped from him and his hands dropped from his throat and onto his chest. Finally one of her tormentor's was dead; soon she would be free of the other one forever. She stepped over his body and walked out onto the landing, as she walked down the staircase she had only one thought in her mind. She walked into the living room and stood in the middle of the floor facing her grandmother's chair. Her grandmother looked up and snarled, "Go back to bed."

Helena levelled the gun at her and said, "You knew all this time what he was doing to me. You knew and you didn't stop him. You let him abuse me and you said nothing grandmother. Why did you not help me, why? It doesn't matter now anyway because he will abuse me no more." Her grandmother sat in stunned silence when she realised that Helena had already killed her grandfather. Two more shots rang out in quick succession and ripped through her grandmother's chest.

Helena let the gun slip from her hand and fall heavily on the floor; the second part of her plan had worked beautifully. She went to the hallway and slipped on her coat, she had decided to join her friends to enjoy the fireworks after all.

The following morning Helena put the third part of her plan into practice; she called the police and told them that she had killed her grandparents. She sat motionless in the kitchen as the sound of sirens blared in the distance and came audibly closer. She opened the door to the two policemen who had raced to the scene hoping to find that it was a hoax. The devastation that greeted their eyes told them that the little girl's call was for real. Her grandparents lay where they had died and it was clear that they had been defenceless when they were gunned down. One of the officers looked at the slight young girl and wondered how such a beautiful young girl could do such a thing...he would not have long to wait for his answer. With tears streaming down her face she shouted at the top of her voice, "You should not have done the things you did to me grandfather!" Then pointing to the body of her grandmother she said, "You knew what he was doing but you didn't stop him. Why grandmother. Why?"

It didn't take a genius to work out exactly what the motive behind the killings was; but they were investigating officers and not a jury. The house was sealed off and a team of forensics were called as Helena was formally arrested and taken into protective care. A psychiatrist was assigned to her and soon the full extent of her ordeal, the horrendous life this young girl had suffered at the hands of her grandparents was brought to light. For her own health and safely it was decided by the authorities to place her in a closely guarded children's home, where she stayed until she was eighteen years of age after which she was placed in an adult mental institution.

Over the course of the two years in the institution, Helena learned many other things. She learned to pretend that she was sorry for killing her grandparents and she learned to stay quiet whenever anyone was looking at her through the grill on her door. She would pretend she was reading. She gave such a good impression that she was no longer a threat to a herself or society that by the time she reached the age of twenty, discussions were taking place to release her into a society that she was not yet ready for, but in which she intended to survive any way she could...

# Chapter Eight

Helena stirred in her sleep and awoke to the sound of birds singing in the trees. Stretching her lithe young body, she got out of bed and looked out of her bedroom window. The weather had been wet and cold of late so she was pleased to see such a fine morning.

She had been out on her own for six months now and still could not get fully used to the fact she could go where she wanted, whenever she wanted. No longer was she kept in a room where there were bars on the windows and a grill on the locked door. No more did she have to sit in front of a psychiatrist listening to endless pointless questions about what she feels about the past. *Surely it is my future you people should be interested in?* Still. There is no point in dwelling on those dark years—not on a morning as glorious as this—now she didn't have to pretend that she was recovered enough to be considered for release.

She padded through to the kitchen and made herself a cup of coffee. She would plan her day as she showered, she always felt invigorated as the water found its course over her body. She stood in the shower mesmerised as the water escaped in its tiny vortex as she juxtaposed the sight before her with the wasted years of her young life.

Six months earlier, she had been released into society after having been found a basement flat in the middle of a bustling city. The flat consisted of a lounge, kitchen, bathroom, and a bedroom. It was decorated in a nondescript manner and one befitting a halfway house between the institution and the *real* world. There were no colours that could be considered 'angry' everything was either cream or magnolia and that included the carpets on each floor. All in all, it appeared to be a comfortable basement. Helena had already met and became friendly with several of the other tenants in the building. She soon gathered that they had not been briefed by the authorities that the flat belonged to the mental institution, so she thought it best not to volunteer the information. After all, people could be *strange* about things like that. It didn't

45

matter too much anyway because she preferred her own company and especially so at night.

Helena remembered her dreams of when she was younger and her ambitions of becoming a professional person. Wanting to be a doctor or solicitor was going to be hard work and would involve many years of study, but it would also give her lots of opportunities. She had plans to make, plans for her future and plans for the rest of her life. One thing she knew for certain was that never again would she allow any man to take advantage of her. Never again would she allow her body to be used to satisfy a man's lust. Men were evil, they were created in the devil's own image and she would rather die than allow one to touch her again...which by default meant that she would also kill rather than allow a man to touch her. That was one thing she cleverly managed to conceal from the relentless probing of her psychotherapist. She drove those thoughts to the back of her mind because today she had other plans to make, she was nearing her 21$^{st}$ birthday and she planned to have a party, only the second party in her life, but this one was going to be so different.

She had not known that her grandparents had left a will, ironically that will was totally in her favour and the circumstances in which she killed them did not affect what was a perfectly legal document. It was discovered that the grandparents had been reasonably wealthy and, although they preferred to stay in the house that their daughter was born in, they could so easily have afforded something bigger. Her grandfather had invested shrewdly in several construction companies that were engaged in the rebuilding of the bombed out German cities. These facts were discovered very soon after Helena was institutionalised and the money she was to inherit would be hers on reaching 21 years of age.

The sun was shining on the 16$^{th}$ March 1961 and, although it was still the last few days of the winter, it was quite warm. Helena awoke and wrapped her arms about herself, the day was a milestone in her life that she never thought she would reach...she had officially become a woman. She was young, healthy and although she did not know it then, she would soon be comparatively well off.

She dressed that morning casually in jeans and sweater and decided to take a long walk, to celebrate her freedom and her maturity into womanhood. She left the flat and turned left intending to walk into town. She had barely walked 100 yards when a sharp pain shot through her head and made her stop. The pain was so bad that it almost blinded her; she held herself up against a wall and waited a few minutes to steady herself before she carried on walking.

Half an hour later, she was in the centre of town and standing outside the offices of her solicitor. She had received a letter a few days previously requesting her to attend the office on the morning of her 21$^{st}$ birthday so she was eager to learn what was in store for her. Two hours later, she left the solicitors office in the full knowledge she was a wealthy young woman with the whole world before her. No amount of money could compensate for the cruelty of her grandmother and the torture she endured at the hands of her grandfather and her immediate thoughts were to tell the solicitor that she did not want their money. However, her common sense prevailed, rejecting the money would not be hurting anyone and the only person to suffer would be herself. No, she would not accept the money as compensation for the way she had suffered at their hands, but she would accept it as payment for the years she served behind bars for killing them and the thought suddenly became all the sweeter.

At home, Helena sat alone in the silence of her living room and she began to form her plans, one of which would—if she was clever enough not to get caught—leave six innocent men dead. Suddenly, the unholy pain that had almost floored her earlier in the morning shot once again through her head, the same pain as before yes, but this time it was far more severe and it lasted a few minutes longer. Over the next hour the pain deepened in intensity and length, at one point she felt as if her head would burst. The pain reached a climax which made her cover her eyes with her hands to keep out even the faintest hint of light. Over time the

47

pain eased and before she knew it she fell asleep...it was then that the dreams began.

She is walking along a road and she comes to a labyrinth of alleyways. Walking along one of the alleys, she realises that she has come full circle and ended back at the beginning. Somewhere in her head, a memory stirred, she has seen this alley before, she is confused and turns all the way round, but nothing else happens. Her dream fades away and Helena is left sleeping peacefully until she awakens with no trace of the excruciating headache. She recalls her dream and thinks about it for a while after which she puts it away in her memory where it will stay...until the next time.

# Chapter Nine

The first days of spring are usually chilly, with a crisp early morning frost of rime still on the ground. This spring was no different and Helena decided to make good use of the early morning sunshine. She headed out for a walk in the park to check on the progress of the sprouting crocuses as they pushed their tiny periscopes through the earth and into the sky. She liked to walk with the fresh air all about her; it seemed to clear her head which lately had become full of all kinds of kaleidoscope thoughts. She needed a clear head for what she intended to do. She had plans to make for the coming months, ideas that would need an exceptional amount of precision planning if they were to stand any chance of success.

Before very long she had walked through the park and into the centre of town. She had a perfunctory look around the shops and bought a few bits and pieces she needed before deciding to take the long way home. As she walked, she came to an alleyway which she hadn't really noticed before. Thinking it could be a shortcut she thought it deserved further exploration so she walked along its length. Only when she reached the other end did she realise she had come full circle. *This is so strange, I'm sure I've seen something like this before, but I can't remember where.*

She walked home hoping to stroll through familiar gardens and take in the pleasant scenes that a warm spring day had to offer. Suddenly she was sickened by the most disgusting stench that seemed to pervade the air about her. Up ahead she saw that a machine was over a manhole cover in the road. A man stood above the hole with a long line of rods that he was obviously using to unblock the sewer. Even though the smell emitting from the hole was horrendous she couldn't resist taking a closer look. As she neared the machine she saw another man dressed in brightly coloured oilskins emerging from the manhole. She stood and watched him for a while totally mesmerised, until she realized that the workmen were beginning to stare at her. As she moved on, thoughts crept into her head and a piece of her jigsaw that had been troubling her for a while suddenly clicked into place, she had found the perfect place to put her plans into operation.

Back at her flat she went over some early notes that she had made of her plans. There were so many details that had to be worked out to ensure everything went right and if anything should go wrong, she had the perfect alibi. If she made her plans well then she would never get caught, but she knew there was a fine line between excellence and arrogance. However, one thing was for sure, she now knew where her victims would go once they were dead.

Nerves racked through her body as she prepared to put the first phase of her plan into operation. She was wise enough to know that first she must choose her victims very carefully. They would have to be a certain kind of man as it would be improper to just kill the first man she encountered. As she began to put the finishing touches to her meticulous plans she was suddenly seized by the pains she had earlier. The pains gripped her head so badly that on this occasion she passed out banging her head on the table as she fell. There she stayed still and unconscious for over an hour. When she eventually came to she struggled to remember where she was or what she had been doing. There was no hint of the pain but she felt strange. Without moving from the chair she looked all around her to establish that she was still in her own flat. For a moment she thought she was back in the institution. The past few days had been very strange. There had been periods when Helena could not remember the simplest things and she had begun to suffer flashbacks from her childhood all times of the day or night, a frightening pattern had begun to emerge. The blinding headaches had begun to occur more often, yet when she slept, she dreamt the same dream and the pain went away. Helena finally pushed herself up off the chair and crawled on her hands and knees to her bed. No sooner had she laid her head on the pillow when the dream began again, the same never ending alleyway, the difference being that this time the dream lasted a little longer.

She walked the same alleyway coming full circle, but on her second walk, she was halfway along the alley when a door suddenly appeared in the brickwork. Try as she might, she could not open the door, so she decided that it must be locked, she left it and walked on. By the time she completed the second circuit, the dream had begun to fade away and Helena completed her sleep peacefully. No more dreams that night.

The next morning dawned bright and clear. As it was early spring, there was still a slight frost in the air, but the crispness of the morning suited Helena very well. Fully recovered from her attack of the previous day with the help of a sound sleep Helena went about her flat with a revitalised sense of purpose.

The day was a new day, a new beginning and the start of her plans for only one possible future. Today she would begin her search for her first victim; the only problem was, *Where shall I begin?*

# Chapter Ten

Night brings the ear splitting screams of a man in the throes of death, yet in the cold light of day, all is peaceful and quiet.

These are the thoughts that flash through Helena's brain. She imagines the moment when she kills her first man. She feels the shivers of excitement run down her spine and a tingling feeling in her fingers as she wraps them around the handle of the kitchen knife on the table in front of her. As she picks up the knife and twirls it around in her hands, she finds it hard to tear her eyes away from the sleek beauty of its shining blade.

She feels the thrill of thrusting the knife into the belly and twisting it round and round, then pulling the knife out and watching as the blood spills down his stiffened legs and into the gutters, to mix with the rain that will soon flood the stinking sewers... his final resting place! She listens intently to the stifled screams of the man—rather like a connoisseur of music might commit a lyrical phrase to the indelible vault of his mind—as he eventually falls to the ground almost dead. Killing a man was not easy, it had taken several minutes for the man to fall and Helena was beginning to wonder if he would ever stop kicking. In the end the struggle was worth it, she looked down at his weak, defenceless carcass crumpled at her feet and she raised the blood covered blade, made black by the moonlight once more above her head but she does not strike the final blow. The drama must be lived to the full; the rain falls gently as Helena stands like a warrior queen and waits for her vanquished enemy to draw his last breath. Eventually he succumbs to the blood loss as his life finally ebbs away. With the strength of ten men high on adrenalin and bloodlust Helena watches herself lift the drain cover and push his body down into the sewer—more food for the rats. She pulls the cover back over the manhole and stands looking at it not believing she has actually killed her first man.

Helena is brought out of her reverie by the return of the crushing pain shooting through her head. This pain is much worse than any pain she has felt before. The pain is so bad she is paralysed and she fights to rise from her chair. Eventually she makes it to her bed by clawing her way along the floor. The moment she lies on the bed, the pain begins to fade and the dream begins again.

The never ending alleyway, the door which is not locked but will not open, but this time, when Helena looks behind her, there is a shadow coming along the alleyway, but Helena is not worried by this…not yet. She continues her walk along the alleyway and once again it ends at the beginning. Halfway along the alley, she comes to the same door. When she looks behind her the shadow has moved a little further along the wall and is a little closer to her than before. Now she begins to feel anxious and tries to open the door.

Eventually the door opens and Helena steps through. She leans against the wall to catch her breath with her eyes closed. A few minutes later, she opens her eyes and finds herself back in her own room and bed. Once again the dream has faded and the pain has gone. The memory of the dream has remained with Helena. She thinks about it for a few minutes trying desperately to figure out what it all means. Never before has she had the feeling that she was being followed. She does not understand how at first the door would not open and, when it eventually does, what is the significance of the second alleyway. The thing that she needed to identify was the shadow creeping along the wall.

Helena has recovered enough to find that she is both hungry and thirsty. She realizes that the day has turned to night and it is growing dark outside. As she prepares herself a meal, her thoughts turn to the dream she has just experienced. She finds it strange that she should be in a second alleyway. Where does it lead to? What is at the end of the alley, if there is an end, but does it run full circle as the first one does? Questions, questions, questions but as yet, there were no answers to those questions.

As she sits at her table prodding at her meal with her fork, her mind drifts back to the dream. She remembers the ghostly shadow following her along the wall. She asks herself the question, *What does that shadow mean? It must signify something, but what?* All these questions are too much for her and she resolves to try to put them out of her mind and enjoy what is left of the night. To clear her head, she goes for a walk but it's not long before that shadow invades her thoughts again. Without fully realizing it— almost trance like—Helena finds herself in the centre of town and at the beginning of the alley she has just been dreaming about. She stands at the entrance and looks along its length; she is baffled by the fact that there doesn't seem to be an ending. She can not separate the dream from reality and she is afraid of both. She wonders what would happen if she went to the exit and began her walk from there? Would that identify the shadow?

Soon she hears the church bells ringing out at Midnight and she decides to return home. Rain has begun to fall softly causing little rivulets to run into the sewers and she is mesmerised as she watches the water drain away. She thinks of the blood that will soon be running down those same drains and her gait quickens. A curious smile etches on her face as all thoughts of the shadow have evaporated into the silence of the night.

Helena reached home and robotically enters her flat. Gently closing the door behind her, she leaned against it and her mind drifted away to some other place. Thirty minutes later, she opened her eyes expecting to see her own room, instead she finds herself at the beginning of the alley back in the centre of town. *But this is impossible!* Looking around wildly, she wonders how in Heavens name she got there. She begins to stumble on into the alley hoping to find once and for all the identity of the shadow that is tormenting her and playing with her mind. As usual she comes to the same door as before, but this time, there is a difference. This time it opens easily allowing her access to the next alley. She looks around her wondering which path to take when she sees that the shadow has followed her into this second alley. She begins to walk away from the shadow and eventually realises that no matter how fast she walks, that shadow is always with her. She begins to be afraid and tries to hurry along, hoping to reach the end. This alley appears to be shorter and narrower than the first one, but in front of Helena, there are two doors. She wonders which one to choose. She feels there is significance in there being two doors, what that significance is, she has yet to discover.

As she closes her eyes to think, she begins to tremble uncontrollably. She wraps her arms around herself against the cold settling on her body. When she eventually opens her eyes, she is once again in her own home. She allows her eyes to close again as a tremendous fatigue grips her body. At last, she feels she can relax without the feeling of dread as to where she will end up. Suddenly she sits up and stares around the room...still there are more questions and no answers filling her already bursting mind. Finally—in complete exhaustion—she falls asleep and for the first time in a long time, she sleeps a full and dreamless sleep, awakening refreshed the next morning.

# Chapter Eleven

Helena lies on the psychiatrist's couch, and recalls the events that eventually lead to her first killing. The psychiatrist watches as her face changes from calm, peaceful and beautiful, into the face of pure evil. If not for his training he would have had no idea that someone so young and pretty could even contemplate the evil that she has done. It felt so strange to him, watching and waiting for her to speak, yet fearing her next words not knowing what scenes of evil she was about to create.

She wakes from a peaceful night's sleep and attunes herself to the sounds of the morning. She stretches her body being careful to commit each move to memory so that she can recall each and every second of the day. Her dark eyes move purposefully over to the window. As she rises from her bed and looks out of the window, she sees the sun shining brightly and it promises to be a beautiful day once again. *Good, beautiful killings deserve such beautiful days.* She walks into her bathroom and takes a long hot shower. As the water flows over the perfect curves of her body she dreams of how the events of the day will unfold. Suddenly, she is back at the alley with two doors. On the wall opposite, she sees the shadow. She knows that it has no eyes and yet she somehow knows that it is looking at her. Thankfully it has not ventured any closer. She watches it, and continues to do so as she slowly moves toward the two doors. Finally, taking a chance, she takes her eyes away from the shadow and takes hold of the right hand side door handle. She twists and turns it, but it will not open. She is concentrating on trying to open the door and does not notice the shadow slowly making its move along the wall toward her. Finally giving up on the door, she turns and sees the shadow is almost upon her. Vulnerable in her nakedness she panics and a cold sweat begins to pour down her face and neck. Somehow she sees her own face looking back at her with a look of indescribable horror which has contorted its beauty into a grotesque death mask. She runs to the left hand door. Still panic-stricken she cannot move the door handle. Twist as she might it will not budge and it takes her some time to realise that the door is in fact already open. She eventually goes through the door and closes it behind her. Tentatively, she looks along the alley and there is the shadow. Its face is becoming clearer. Helena can now see the red, blood-shot eyes and its other demonic features. She turns ghostly white, puts her hands to her mouth to stop herself from screaming and opens her eyes to find herself back in the shower.

Helena's daily routine is breakfast first, which consists of nothing more than black coffee. She finds that it somehow sustains her for most of the day. As the sun is shining and the day is beginning to warm up, she decides to go somewhere to gather her thoughts; a change of environment is what she needs. She dressed casually in jeans and a t-shirt and she sets out with a feeling of pessimism. She has nothing else in mind but perhaps an enjoyable day at the beach people watching and relaxing by the sea.

Arriving at the popular seaside resort, she finds that there are already a number of families with the same idea. Mothers sat and chatted to each other as the children played in the water and built sandcastles. Fathers showed their sons how to strike a football properly even though they had no clue. Usually the sons were infinitely better and every now and then one would collapse in fits of laughter as the father miss-kicked the ball and it went in entirely the wrong direction. There were ice cream vendors selling their mouth-watering goods and plenty of fun; what a glorious day it was going to be.

Helena sat on the stone wall of the promenade and watched the scenes around her. Her mind began to wander back into the past. With all those smiling children about her it was only going to be a matter of time before the days of her childhood surfaced and with them came all the things she regretted. All the childhood she should have had, all the things she missed and suffered suddenly flooded into her thoughts. Life back then had been very bleak and there had been so much pain and suffering, events in a young girl's life that should never have happened. It was too late to do anything about those events now, but what was in her control was the rest of her life. She could decide the way the rest of her life would turn. She was brought out of her reverie by the sound of a man's voice close to her. Very slowly, she turned to look at the man sitting next to her. She said: "I'm sorry. I didn't realise that you were talking to me. What were you saying?"

The man looked at her with a furrowed brow, "I was just wondering why you were crying", he replied as he offered her his handkerchief to wipe away her tears. Helena had not realised she was crying, she wiped the tears from her face. As she thanked him for his kindness and concern she said: "It is nothing really, just nostalgia, I was looking at all these children at play and thinking back to the time my grandparents were killed." The young man began to ask her questions about her grandparents. Too many questions for a man she had only just met and it made her feel uncomfortable. She got up, made her excuses and walked away, leaving the young man staring after her. The idea of a trip to the beach to gather her thoughts was—on reflection—perhaps not the best one she could have had.

Two days of self-imposed imprisonment elapsed and Helena found herself sat in her kitchen staring blankly into space. Suddenly a pain shot through her head, it was so severe that she slipped from the chair and collapsed to the floor. In between bouts of semi-consciousness she attempted to crawl to her bed. This time she did not succeed so she stayed where she had fallen. The best she could do was to painfully reach behind her, pulling the rug over her to give herself some semblance of warmth. The pain became so intense that she passed out completely and there she stayed.

If she had known what evil was waiting for her in the depths of her unconscious mind, she would have forced herself to stay awake…the moment she was asleep…the dream began. It had happened so many times, so she knew what was going to happen. She was not prepared however, for the ensuing events. As she stepped through the door, the first thing she noticed was that this alley seemed to be shorter than the last, although it was still as wide. Looking to her right, she noticed that the shadow was still there, but there were no other changes in its appearance. She turned her back on the shadow and began walking in the opposite direction. Her mind was beginning to ask questions which in turn made her more than a little nervous. Why so many alleys, the changes in the shadow, the doors that refuse to open? All these questions that Helena had no answers to; she did not know it then, but with the answers would come an evil that the world could never comprehend. In her sleep, she screams silently as an ungodly hand reaches out and slowly envelopes her entire being. She awakens in her own room, still on the floor, her face covered in a cold, clammy sweat and she was still wrapped up in the rug.

She shivers as a sudden chill crawls painfully slowly down the full length of her spine. Lying motionless in the dark silence for several minutes she wills herself to move but all she can muster is the strength to get shakily to her feet. She managed to stumble over to the sink and turned the cold tap on full to splash water onto her burning face. Turning from the sink she forced herself to focus on the steps she would have to take to make it over to the sofa. Slowly, purposefully placing one foot in front of the other she walked to the sofa and slumped down to gather her thoughts. *The shadow on the wall, the face with no eyes, the third alley, all of these things must mean something.* There had to be a reason for all the things happening to her. How many alleys will there finally be? Will the shadow ever catch her and what will happen if it does? One thing she knew for certain was that the plans for her first kill were almost complete and she even had her first victim in sight. The only thing left was to choose the right time and place to ensure the first execution was a total...and bloody success.

Thinking back to the young man on the promenade, Helena was certain that he was taken with her; why else would he take such an interest? She intended to cultivate the friendship to find out for sure. Maybe she should return to the beach tomorrow, he may be there again? Excitement began to course through her body when she thought of what lay tantalisingly ahead of her. The fear and heaviness of her nightmares gradually gave way to daydreams and as she regained her strength she found herself standing at the kitchenette with a blade in her hand. She was turning and twisting the knife round and round in her hand totally mesmerised by the gruesome smoothness of the blade and more menacingly…what she could do with it and the pain she could inflict.

With that thought in mind she slid the knife back into its place and made her way to bed. For the task ahead she was going to need a good night's sleep and, hopefully, without dreams. There was so much she needed to prepare herself for. As she settled down beneath the comfort of her blankets she began to imagine all kinds of wonderful endings for the coming event; how she would keep him alive and conscious until the last thing he ever saw was the smile of sweet satisfaction on her face. Besides the moment of death there were other more mundane plans to make, would she change the scenario one last time or would she go with the plan that had been so successful in her mind? She settled on the conclusion that she would be best following her original plan, that way there would be no evidence and besides, rats may not be the nicest rodents, but they still had to eat.

Helena awoke the next morning to find the sun shining through the gap in the curtains. She climbed out of bed and peered into the shaft of light at the clear blue sky. *Today is going to be a beautiful day in more ways than one.* She showered and dressed quickly and soon she was ready to go; her destination, the place where the sight of her tears had seduced the knight in shining armour.

She hardly noticed the journey to the sea as the train punched its way through the glorious sunshine like a great snorting stallion. She was focused on what was about to take place and the excitement coursed through her veins like molten lead. On arriving at the seaside, she found that there were lots of people already around. Families sat on the beach, parents sitting together talking whilst the children played. The sounds of children laughing as they played in the sand—a sound she had not heard since she was a child. She sat on the promenade and watched fascinated as the parents began setting out picnics on large blankets laid out on the sand as lunchtime approached. Her face was suddenly pained with sadness as she remembered her lost childhood. Thoughts of the first and only party she ever had rose in the form of impressionist pictures in her brain.

It hurt so deeply to see grandparents having such fun with their grandchildren and it made her think of the grandparents she had been forced to kill. Her mind drifted back to a time when her grandfather was everything to her, back then, when she was nine years old, she thought he was the greatest person in the entire world. Almost all of what she ever learned came from her grandfather and now she was an adult, she began to realise that he had taught her far more things than learning to read and write. He had, in fact, been training her in all aspects including the adult side of life. Back then, before the devastation, there had been no indications of the monster her grandfather was to become.

She sat on the promenade wall watching the children play until she realised that she was looking for a man she knew nothing about. *What if he had been here on a day trip on that day?* As the sun began to sink into the western sky and the families made their way back up the beach and away from the advancing tide Helena too joined in the exodus and headed back into the town. She stopped at a terrace café in the late afternoon sunshine, and as she looked at the menu she heard a familiar voice. "What would be your heart's desire madam?" Slowly lifting her eyes the voice went on, "Those eyes are still sad, but not as sad as the last time I saw them." She couldn't believe that the waiter was the man she had been looking for. He smiled at her and Helena's sad eyes smiled back at him. "It's nice to see you again, although I was beginning to think I never would," he said, "My name is Carl, what's your name?"
Helena offered her hand, "Helena Maria Schultz", she smiled, "And my heart desires that you sit and talk to a lonely girl with sad eyes."

"I finish here in half an hour, why don't you have a drink until then and I will show you all the delights of my town, starting with dinner for two at an exquisite French restaurant?"

"What would you recommend?" Helena teased.

"Hmm, something long and luxuriously cool with a subtle hint of spice and a bite that would make you tingle all over," he whispered out of earshot of the other customers. "What sort of drink is that?" Helena asked.

"It is not a drink Helena, it is me," he smiled.

"In that case, bring me a strong coffee; I want to be wide awake later so that I don't miss a thing."

With that Carl turned on his heels and brought her a coffee which she sipped seductively until he was ready to escort her on a tour of *his* town.

The restaurant was indeed exquisite, the dimly lit ambience was the perfect setting for a burgeoning romance and Carl was the epitome of charm and charisma. For him Helena oozed sexuality from every pore and her delightful conversation so richly complimented the meal. All too soon the evening was at an end; the sun was beginning to set on the horizon and parents were gathering their children preparing to leave the beach and the town for another year. Carl asked Helena where she was staying and when he learned that she was only there for the day he asked if he could see her home.

"But I live miles away," Helena laughed.

"For one more moment with you I would walk to the ends of the earth," he smiled. Helena knew that it was more than just a show of friendship. She was not yet ready to cultivate a romance. The painful memories of her childhood were still too real for her. To Carl, for her to say yes was an invitation to share Helena's life, he had thought of no one else since he first laid eyes on her so long ago.

He should not have been so eager, he had no way of knowing of the unspeakable danger his invitation would put him in before the sun was to rise again. As they walked to the train station Helena slipped her arm through his and linked him. To an unknowing onlooker they were the picture of new romance, a couple strolling through the sweet scented twilight over ancient cobbled streets. Helena clung to every word as Carl talked about his life and his family. The mood began to change when Carl innocently asked about Helena's family. She deftly changed the subject by suggesting they talk of the future rather than the past to which Carl agreed. Helena let her head fall onto his shoulder as they made their way to the station, he liked the feeling and he filled his senses with the intoxicating perfume of her hair. His hand rested on her shoulder as he held her closer to his body, his heart was already pounding at the thought of what lay ahead. Helena's heart too was beating faster with every step towards their destination…but her heart beat so furiously for a very different reason.

# Chapter Twelve

As the late evening set in the couple wound their way along the riverside, which was so pleasant and peaceful. Everything is beautiful in the very first stages of a relationship, where silences are quickly filled with small talk. It was at that time of night when there are no distractions except perhaps for the odd cat crying like a baby in the distance. Carl commented on how nice it was listening to the soft breezes among the trees and the final throes of bird song as they settle down to roost. Their talk was general and covered many subjects but every time Carl mentioned Helena's family she was reluctant to talk about them and she changed the subject. Before they realised it, night had fallen. There was no moon that night, so apart from the few stars that shone dimly in the night sky and the few street lights that were lit... they were enveloped in complete darkness.

Helena turned a corner and, without him realising it, she led Carl onto the road back toward town. He carried on with his small talk with an ever growing confidence that the night was going to lead to something special. As they walked Helena fingered the handle of the heavy blade in her pocket and the excitement of what she knew was about to happen coursed through her veins. He was not to know that she had a knife in that pocket and that that hand was making sure it stayed there until she was ready to use it. She was a long way off showing that hand yet. There were other things that needed to be done before the night was over. She wanted to tease every ounce of his stupidity out of him before her knife found its willing target. She slowed down when they came to a bench by the side of the road. "Shall we sit here a while and enjoy this beautiful evening Carl?" she whispered seductively, "Oh how I wish I could make time stand still." She wanted the thrill of what was about to happen to last as long as possible. Carl smiled at the romance hidden within the gesture, he knew that Helena was setting the scene so that he could steal a kiss and he sat down beside her. He gazed into her eyes and saw that tell-tale sparkle that meant she liked him. How wrong could he

64

have been? The smile on her face was the delight she was creating in her mind, thinking of his imminent death. He put his hands in his pockets and, with a sheepish look on his face, sat down on the bench beside her. They sat in silence for several minutes looking up at the glittering stars in the deep cerulean blue night before Helena suggested they walk back to her flat. Carl's heart skipped a beat because from there on every step would take him closer to the paradise he had been waiting for. Helena carried on with her relentless teasing suggesting they take the long way round. She casually whispered that she has found a very interesting alley he may like the look of. An interesting alley was the last thing on his mind but he didn't let his eagerness ruin the moment. "What could be so interesting about an alley?" he asked.

"This is no ordinary alley, it goes full circle and you end at the beginning after just a few strides." Helena smiled. Carl did not believe that such an alley existed but he played along with her teasing by insisting they go there at once. Helena giggled like a child and took him by the hand as she led him to what will be... his death.

The walk to the alley took about twenty minutes but time passed quickly as they chattered about sweet nothings. They finally arrived at the alley and Helena led Carl to the very beginning. She stopped and let go of his hand and took several minutes to point out a few noticeable things that she knew Carl would recognise easily before they set off along the alley. It was absolutely pitch black along the alley; there were no street lights anywhere along its length. Helena pretended to be afraid of the dark so that Carl would offer his hand like a gentleman to lead her. Halfway along the alley he stopped and pulled Helena close to him, he could feel her warm breath on his face, it was the moment he had longed for since the very first time he saw her beauty. He wrapped his arms tightly around her and kissed her passionately on the lips, Helena's body went limp in his arms and he knew that she was his. One kiss turned into another, longer embrace as Helena eagerly returned his kisses. They pulled apart just long enough to catch their breath; Helena puts her finger against his lips, "No, not here Carl, I want this to be so very special," she whispered breathlessly. Carl took her hand once more to lead her to the end of the alley. Yes they have come full circle but Carl has other things on his mind. A streetlight loomed out of the blackness and they stood beneath it, safe in the warmth of its protective glow. Carl told Helena that he had lived in that town all his life and never knew that the alley existed. Helena looked at her watch and cursed inwardly at the hours it had stolen, it was almost 1am. She wanted everything to be perfect. The chase had gone like a dream; here he was beside her and almost begging to be slain. The lead up to the end had been beautiful in the way that Carl was romantic and behaved like a doe-eyed puppy, *and they say that women are the weaker sex? Look at him, the pathetic fool doesn't even know that he has less than an hour to live and he is planning a lifetime with me. Well that part of his dream is about to come true.* "Let's go home," she whispered seductively. She slid her arm in his once again and they begin the final few hundred yards to her home. The night was cool and blue and made for lovers. After a few yards Helena stopped abruptly.

"What is it?" Carl asked.

"Over there by the doorway, I saw someone," Helena whispered.

Carl peered into the darkness ahead of him, "Wait here, I will take a look." He moved slowly and quietly towards the blackened doorway and looked tentatively inside. He was about to turn and let Helena know that her eyes were playing tricks on her when suddenly his breath was punched from his lungs by a devastating pain in his lower back. His mouth opens to scream in agony but the sound is trapped in his throat. Wide eyed he staggers back from the doorway and turned to find Helena standing in front of him with a knife in her hand, the gruesome blade dripping great globs of blood down onto the pavement. The shock on his face and the look of confusion in his eyes is asking why she has stabbed him. Instead of an answer, he got the cold blade of the knife rammed into his belly and twisted several times before being pulled out again. With a look of pained confusion etched onto his face he tried to hold his intestines in as he sank down to his knees. Helena coolly watched as his life slowly ebbed away before her eyes.

"Why?" Carl whispered with his dying breath.

"For my beautiful mother," she grinned, "when you meet her, tell her I sent you as a gift from me. I will send my father a different sacrifice."

Carl slumped into the gutter and watched helplessly as his blood drained away. There was nothing he could do to stop it. Helena seemed oblivious to the fact that someone else might pass that way. Instead she stared with a childlike fascination at the blood on the blade which looked jet black in the moonlight. She stepped over him and smiled a sadistic smile as his bewildered dying eyes stared up at her questioningly. In her mind his screams split the silence of the night as she brought the knife into his view and although he was all but dead she sliced his throat from ear to ear. With a harrowing, guttural gurgling sound Carl Schmitt was dead. As the last of his blood disappeared down the drain, washed away by the rain, Helena, calmly put the knife back inside her coat. Only then did she look around to check if she had been seen. Part of her wanted to stay with a consuming urge to admire her night's work. Part of her knew that she had to leave because sooner or later someone would make the grim discovery. *I hope the rats have the chance to feed on you before morning, that way your miserable life will have been worthwhile.*

With that Helena calmly began the walk home. It was going to take her a long time to come down from the incredible high of bloodlust and satisfaction. The thrill she felt as the knife went into Carl's stomach was unbelievable. She realised she was shaking with the sheer joy of everything she had done. It was planned with minute precision and executed with such glorious passion.

She wanted to scream at the top of her voice to let the world know what she had done. The sheer ecstasy she felt at her first kill since she had dispatched her grandparents touched the very core of her being.

67

Finally she made her way home soaked to the skin by the rain that had begun to fall and she closed the door behind her. Resting for a few minutes against the closed door, she let out a huge sigh of relief. She knew that very soon she would have to start planning her next kill, but for now all she needed was a good night's sleep so that she could re-live the night in her dreams. She briefly thought about how she might feel when the morning came and the newspapers began to spread terror into the town, but decided she would face that tomorrow, after all, tomorrow was another day.

## Chapter Thirteen

Helena woke from a deep sleep to the sight of her blood stained clothes. At first they repulsed her until she realised that they were the result of her life's ambition. She lifted up the coat and held it to her face as if to caress the deed all over again as if it were a living thing. *Much as it pains me to burn you, it will have to be done.*

She let the coat drop to the floor as she searched the rest of her clothes for any incriminating signs that she had been involved. Finding nothing visible to the naked eye she felt confident that there was no tell-tale evidence that she had been anywhere else last night than tucked up safely in her bed.

Helena dressed quickly and headed out into the morning for a newspaper: being able to read about the kill would make for a special thrill especially as she planned to casually walk by the scene later in the day. Even from a distance she could see that the writing on the bill-board outside the shop was headlining a local murder. On closer inspection she was disgusted to read the line, MAN'S MUTILATED BODY FOUND BY EARLY MORNING DOG WALKER. *The Bastards! He was not mutilated, he was symbolically sacrificed! How dare they use that horrible word, mutilated, to mutilate someone is to kill their parents, to sacrifice someone is to let their blood for the good of others…his blood fed the rats.*

### Some time later

Klaus Bauer stands almost six feet in height, a burly, no-nonsense ex-paratrooper with a steely wit and a character built on giving orders that could potentially cost men their lives, in short, he was a man who thought long and hard before he opened his mouth. The notice on his door reads Dr. K. Bauer, Psychiatrist. It was in this office he sat going over the notes he had made of Helena. While reading the notes, his face twisted into a frown. There are some parts of the notes he does not understand and some parts he can barely come to terms with. Despite his war-time experiences and his training as a psychiatrist he finds the

69

reading un-nerving. Some of the events that have befallen Helena don't seem real at all and yet he knows that every word she has spoken is the absolute truth, under hypnosis...and in her own mind, there is no way she could be telling lies.

While he is waiting for Helena to arrive for her next session, he asks himself the questions he will be putting to her so they must be constructed in a way that she will not feel as though he is trying to judge her, *How did she get away with murder for so long? What motive did she have for killing so randomly? Was it randomly at all? Why did she stop after six men were dead? How did she choose her victims?* Yes he needed answers to all these questions but they would have to be asked over the coming weeks that followed and asked in different ways so that the answers may eventually lead him to the truth...or so his training had taught him.

He had just finished putting his notes back into order when the door opened and Helena walked in. Looking distant and somewhat dishevelled she positioned herself robotically on the couch and was hypnotised within minutes. She is taken back in time to when she met the first of her victims.

The look on Klaus Bauer's face as Helena calmly and without emotion recounted how Carl Schmitt had met his death, spoke volumes. He stopped writing his notes as her story unfolded, it would be better for him he felt, to make mental notes instead so that he could begin the sub-conscious analysis of her state of mind as he went along.

His full attention was on her voice, he was looking for that almost impervious rise in tone that would indicate some level of humanity because the look on her face said that she had enjoyed every minute of the killing, so much so that she could not wait for the second one to happen, yet her voice was cold and flat...it didn't add up. It was as though he was watching and hearing two total strangers at the same time. The smile on her face frightened him enough to make his normally ruddy face turn white as he listened as the gruesome details emerged. Up until now, no-one had known the names of the men who had been murdered. The only thing known was that there had been six possible victims of this seemingly lovely young woman in front of him.

He knew by the ease of her disclosures that with a little more probing he would be able to illicit from her, the names of the other five men and the location of their bodies. He presumed that at this late stage, all that would be left of the victims would be the bleached bones. He was not an expert in that department but the length of time they had been missing would indicate a major form of decay had taken place. Considering how a great number of voracious rats can be when hungry, a human body can be disposed of within minutes. The thought disgusted him as he sat in his chair and stared at the potentially beautiful young woman who was essentially a monster. It took him several moments to bring his attention back to Helena. When he looked at her face again, she suddenly appeared to be gripped by some deep inner anguish. The pain was etched into her face and he knew her well enough to recognise that she was once again in the 'dream zone' as he called it.

Helena checked all around the flat to ensure everything was locked and secure before turning out the lights and going to bed. The elation of the day just finishing was unbelievable. Everything had gone exactly as she imagined it would and she had a satisfied smile on her face as she settled down to sleep. However, hers was not a peaceful sleep. Her head had barely touched the pillow, when the dream began. On the last few occasions, the dream seemed to have started just where it had left off. This time, she was standing in the alley, which seemed to have become shorter, and in front of her there were three doors. She stood absolutely still for several minutes just looking at the doors in front of her. There were several differences about these doors. Whereas before the doors had been plain wooden doors, these were black doors with white handles and each of the doors stood about two feet apart. Slowly turning her head to the right, she notices that the shadow has receded a little but its face is becoming clearer. Now visible are its eyeless sockets and the shape of its nose. The rest of its face is nothing but a blur. What she can see of the face somehow seems familiar to her, but at the moment she is not sure where she knows it from.

Slowly turning her head back to the doors in front of her, she has learned that she must make a choice of which door to open. She knows that this life is made up of choices, so the door she eventually chooses will decide which path her life takes from now on. She also knows from experience, that only two of the doors will open, but intends to try them all anyway, she suspects that it will be the middle door which will be locked. She stands a few minutes longer before finally choosing the door directly in front of her. Walking slowly toward it she hesitated for the briefest fleeting moment before putting her hand on the handle. Then, snapping her closed fist over it she begins twisting it to the right.

She closed her eyes as the handle turned. She is apprehensive of what is behind the door. The handle turns and suddenly Helena opens her eyes not knowing what to expect. She finds herself back in her own room, sitting in her own bed and wide awake. The frustration she felt at not being able to see what was behind the door shows in her face. She screams out at the top of her lungs and bangs her fists on each side of the bed. It takes several minutes for her to calm down and eventually get out of bed. She sits on the edge of her bed with her head in her hands and weeps. It has been so long since she last cried that she had forgotten how good it felt to wash all the frustrations away. Eventually she realised that she had been crying for her lost childhood and the loneliness she felt was overpowering...*perhaps that is what was locked behind that door?*

Helena made her way slowly into the kitchen and made herself a strong black coffee. She took it back to her bedroom and sat on the bed. Wrapping her hands around the mug, she drifted off into a daydream where she saw herself planning the next execution. She knew that the time had come to begin the next phase of her plan and, although a lot of the same method would be used, there was still a lot of planning to be done. Resting her head against the wall behind the bed she closed her eyes for several minutes, when she opened them again she was back in the alley with her hand on the door handle. When she turned the handle the door opened to reveal… absolutely nothing. *How can I have chosen the wrong one again? Yes, that is it! My dreams are giving me a message; why didn't I see it sooner?* Helena was beginning to realise, she had to choose the path either to the left or to the right.

Making choices in life is difficult for everyone. You can never tell if you have made the right choice until the choice you made goes for you or against you. Unfortunately, time cannot be turned back. You have to face your choice, accept the consequences and make the most of it. When Helena is faced with these choices they have an added dimension because there does not seem to be a winning option, at best it is a choice of the lesser of two evils. With that unenviable thought she wonders which door to choose. After a painfully long pause she eventually makes up her mind and advances toward the door on the right. She looked to her right and saw that the shadow has not moved but still its gaze is upon her. It too seems to be curious as to which one she will choose.

Keeping her eyes fixed on the shadow—perhaps mistakenly—she slowly reaches out her hand and takes hold of the door handle. Her hand trembles in trepidation as she begins to put pressure on the handle. She has no idea what is waiting for her behind this door. With her hand slowly increasing the pressure, she momentarily takes her eyes away from the shadow. She feels that the shadow is waiting to pounce on her as she steps through the door. With beads of perspiration running down her neck she pushes the door open and drags her eyes away from the shadow…a momentary sigh of relief escapes involuntarily from her parched lips because the shadow did not pounce. She stepped through the door with her eyes closed. On the far side she sees no alley just a brick wall and in it are five new doors. The thought of more life or death decisions overpowered her and she collapsed in mental exhaustion. She recovers just long enough to find that the door behind her has closed and there is no handle on the inside to get back out. *Yes, that door was the wrong choice, but there is no way back,*

*I have no other choice now but to go forward.* With superhuman strength she raised her aching body and braced herself once more...

## Chapter Fourteen

Klaus Bauer stood up abruptly throwing his pencil and notebook on the table as he did so. He ran to Helena and, taking her by the shoulders shook her hard. She is screaming at the top of her voice despite him trying everything he knew to quieten her but failing miserably. In desperation he slapped her face hard with an immediate response. Staring back at him with the shock of the blow still on her face she realised that she was in no danger and she began to sob. In a soothing voice Bauer took her back into her hypnotic state before safely bringing her back to reality.

"What happened? Where was I?" she whispered pathetically.

"Perhaps you could tell me Helena," Bauer said.

"There was a door," she started. "There was a door..."

"Can you remember what was behind the door?" he asked. Helena's face took on a perplexed look as she tried to recall the dream. Try as she apparently seemed to do she could remember nothing other than the door. Bauer thought for a fleeting moment that she could recall more than she was going to say, but after looking into her eyes and the look of desperation he saw there, he gave her the benefit of the doubt. After several minutes of awkward silence Bauer asked if she was ready to be hypnotised again. He gambled that the suggestion to return might provoke some regaining of her memory loss. She hesitated for an instant before slowly nodding her assent and within minutes she was back at the wall with the five doors in it and Bauer was none the wiser. The last thoughts on Helena's mind as Bauer began the backwards count from 10 to 1 was, *This is my dream and no one will see it until I have lived it out.*

Helena stood with her back against the wall of the alley and very slowly opened her eyes. The doors in front of her have changed in many ways. Whereas before they were five plain wooden doors, these have now got black handles and are painted different colours. Helena looked at the doors with a mixture of awe and childlike fascination. The doors were red, blue, white, green and yellow. She quickly worked out that each different coloured door has a different meaning and as she ran her eyes over each one for some other tell-tale clue she scanned her brain for indicators from her past to help find what the significance could be. She turned to her right hoping this time to see the shadow, but would it still be where it usually was, on her shoulder? She was right, there it was only this time it has a full face now and is grinning at her. *Is it pleased with me I wonder? Perhaps it is my dead father?* She looks again as the grin turns into a familiar sinister smile...she recoiled in horror as she stared into the face of her hated grandmother.

Helena's body trembled with a mixture of fear and anger as she looked into the evil eyes of the grotesque, malevolent face. She struggled with her emotions not knowing whether to run from it or lunge at it to rip it to pieces. The shadow knows only too well that it has Helena scared. *Is this the same, twisted, revenge that I see in those eyes burning with evil, the same eyes that despised everything that didn't reek of death for your enemies?* With enormous effort, Helena managed to pull her gaze back to the doors. Despite the shadow she knew that it had appeared to distract her from the doors. *I know you want to stop me from gaining the knowledge behind these doors, but you never did realise how infinitely stronger than you I was.* Turning from the shadow she concentrates once again on the enigma of the doors. She has no idea why the doors are painted different colours or which one to choose. *The logical place is to start at the beginning,* Helena heads towards the red door. Taking hold of the handle, she turns it and passes through the door thinking as she does so that 'Red is for Blood', Helena likes blood. She is convinced that this door is leading her to her next kill. A smile breaks on her face as she begins to walk along the blood-soaked path in front of her. It has only one direction and once she begins the walk, she cannot turn back. Looking over her shoulder, Helena sees that the door behind her has disappeared. At the far end of the path—which ends all too soon because she can almost taste the blood rising from the ground and she wants to linger—she opens a door and finds she is at home in her own bed. Shaking herself awake, she realises that she now knows when and where her next sacrifice will take place.

With the crooked smile even more evident on her face Helena turned onto her side and snuggled deeper beneath the warm blankets where she instantly fell into a peaceful, dreamless sleep.

Hours later she woke refreshed and stretched her body in a long feline movement. She swung her long legs out onto the floor and padded sleepily through to the bathroom. She looked at her reflection in the mirror and saw that the dark rings under her eyes had all but disappeared. With her inner self assured that her next victim was about to meet his end, a hot shower was all she needed to completely rejuvenate her from the inside out. She threw back her head as the water cascaded over her naked form; she allowed her hands to wander probingly all over her body. Excited at the prospect of what is ahead for her she begins to fondle herself. She moves her fingers faster as her mind closes in on the last moments of her next victim's life and she shudders to one climax after another. As she finally steps from the shower there is only one thing on her mind...putting her plans into action; all she needs is the place and a victim. She already knows that the time will be the dead of night.

Helena looks from her window at the rain sodden morning but nothing could dampen the spirit of sunshine rising in her heart; she decided to take a bus out of town. On the bus she watches the heavy rivulets running down the windows and immediately the rain turns blood red making her smile inwardly as she turned to look at the expressionless faces of her fellow passengers. *Can you not see all this blood? No, but you will read about it soon as you eat your breakfasts.*

Looking back through the window she saw her rain distorted reflection in the glass and began to wonder what significance the face of her grandmother had the last time she saw the shadow. Was she intending to threaten Helena again? Did she intend to hurt her in some way? So many questions to which there were no immediate answers.

Helena reached her destination and stepped lightly off the bus. The rain had given way to some patchy sunshine which looked as though it would not take too long to clear away completely. As the bus drove on by she looked across the road to see a young man standing opposite smiling at her. She returned the smile before turning coyly away. The young man wasted no time in crossing the road to introduce himself... with the corniest chat-up line ever. "Excuse me; don't I know you from somewhere?"

Helena tried not to stare into his piercing blue eyes. He was a womaniser if ever there was one. "I think I would have remembered if we had met before," Helena smiled.

"I know where I know you from, you are the girl from the most beautiful dream I ever had," he said in a fashion resembling a ham actor.

"Is that the best you can do? I would have thought you boys could have thought of a better line than your grandfathers would have used.

He came back at her with a lightning riposte. "I am a traditionalist; I believe the old ones are the best."

She was impressed with the speed of his response but despite his outward confidence she looked into his eyes and realised that she may have hurt his feelings. She offered him another lifeline, "I will give you one more chance to come up with something original."

He looked at her for a moment with a look on his face to suggest that he was going through his full repertoire in his head before he finally said: "I give up, can I buy you a coffee?"

"And what if I say that I am not in the habit of drinking with strangers," she teased.

"Then I would say that my name is Stefan Prem, so we are no longer strangers," he smiled as the confidence returned to his eyes

"In that case I would love to have coffee with you," she smiled.

Stefan led her to a small café just off the main road. It was quiet and the lighting was subdued, it was just right for the intimate small-talk of newly acquainted strangers.

"So what brings you all the way from England to Germany?" Helena asked.

"Is my German that bad that you knew straight away that I am English?"

"I could be kind, but I prefer to be blunt…yes it is!" she laughed.

"Thank you for your honesty, perhaps I should ask for a refund from my teacher," he said in mock disappointment, "I'm a student on a gap year from England. I thought I would travel the world for a while before heading back to university."

Stefan looked to be about the same age as Helena. Over coffee he was charming and witty and he paid her lots of compliments so he wasn't surprised when Helena invited him back to her flat. He gratefully accepted the offer and in less than an hour, they were on the bus heading to her flat. Stealing a look at Helena's face, Stefan thought that the smile he saw was because Helena—like all the others—had fallen for his patter. He had no idea that her seductive smile was the bait and he was the doomed fish.

Helena made a show of going into the kitchen and insisting on cooking him a meal. He protested accordingly in a half-hearted manner until he quickly relented and allowed himself to be fed and watered by the beautiful woman flitting about the flat like a bee in the summer sunshine. He liked the idea that such a beautiful woman was making a fuss of him. The meal and coffee over, the washing up done and put out of the away and then came the moment he had ached for; Helena sat on the sofa beside him. They talked well into the wee, small hours about all the usual things that young lovers find to whisper about. There was soft music in the background and the lighting was perfect for intimacy. Helena managed to keep the subject from turning to her family. They talked of their likes and dislikes until Helena skilfully turned the conversation to his family. It emerged that he had no immediate family to speak of. There was a distant cousin somewhere around England, but no parents, grandparents, brothers or sisters. Helena's interest heightened when she heard that he had grown up in an orphanage. He had been an only child and his parents had both been killed in a car accident when he was about 3 years of age. Both sets of grandparents were long since dead so he had no other family to look after him. Thoughts flashed through Helena's mind that this man was a perfect victim, after all, no-one was going to miss him. Why not give him a little something to think about before he dies? Helena moved closer to Stefan and very quietly whispered that it was time for bed. Stefan looked at Helena and with expert ease took her into his arms and kissed her passionately.

What was left of the night passed in a frenzy of passion and unbridled ecstasy as Helena and Stefan eagerly explored each other's bodies. Helena was not used to the feelings of excitement and raw animal pleasure and she found that she was enjoying every minute of the deep physical contact, so much so that she gives every inch of herself to Stefan. The pleasure was so deep that she even began to regret the fact that he must die. By the time they fell into an entangled exhausted sleep she was past trying to analyse the myriad of feelings and emotions that were coursing through her body.

The following morning Helena was still confused; even more so when Stefan kissed her goodbye with a promise to call her later.

She stood in the kitchen staring blankly at the wall for several minutes after he left. Her mind was swimming in total confusion at what had taken place and her closeness to Stefan. Rather than work things out in her exhausted state she eventually flopped onto her bed and snuggled in amongst the sheets and pillows where the smell of Stefan's body still lingered.

It was a full week before Stefan kept his promise to call her; she knew he would eventually but she had thought that he would have called before that. Nevertheless, the important thing was that he had called and he was eager to meet up again...perfect!

Helena coolly arranged a date for the following night. By then she had had time to clear her head and had no further qualms about killing Stefan. Her plans were already well underway and she knew exactly how his life will be taken from him.

Letting the receiver fall noisily into its cradle she could not help but smile as she began to think of the joys that the next day was going to bring.

With nothing to do but wait she decided to take a walk into town to do some shopping to pass a few hours. Around the centre of town she saw that there were several heavy, cast iron manhole covers in the centre of the road and she wondered how a slight young girl like her might lift one. She would need somewhere safe to dispose of Stefan's body once he was dead.

# Chapter Fifteen

The following night, a full moon shone and a shoal of stars glistened like silver minnows in the darkening sky. Helena liked the stars and she stood at the gate of her basement flat watching them come to life as the evening grew darker. She could have stayed there all night long but for her date with Stefan and she had so much to prepare. She turned to go back into the flat when she saw Stefan walking along the road towards her. He reached the gate and a smile spread across her face as she opened the gate allowing him entry into her world, a world where pleasure, excitement, pain and even death walked hand in hand.

Without a word passing between them she took hold of his hand to lead him into her home and as she did so she looks into his eyes. What she saw there confused her. For the first time in her life she saw genuine trust and love. She did not understand the thoughts and emotions running through her head. She closed the door behind him and walked through to the lounge—the scene of the beginning of such passion the night they first made love. Stefan followed her and, as she turned to face him he put his hands around her waist. Pulling her closer to him, he covered her face with gentle butterfly kisses as his hands run seductively down the middle of her back sending shivers of electric pleasure all the way down. Once again doubts begin to creep into Helena's mind. What should she do? How can she kill this man knowing how much she has grown to love him in the last week and knowing how much he appears to love her? She forced these thoughts to the back of her mind as she pulled away to face him with a smile on her face. "I have a surprise for you my darling," she whispered.

"I just love surprises, am I allowed to guess what you have in store for me?"

"You can guess but you will never be anywhere close," she teased.

As he lifted his eyes to the ceiling in mock pretence at thinking, she began to recall how someone else told her that he loved her and showed it by constantly raping her for three years of her young life. Stefan noticed the sudden change in her demeanour, "Are you alright Helena?"

"Yes why shouldn't I be?" she said defensively immediately wishing she hadn't sounded so curt, "I am just thinking of the last two weeks and how happy I have been," she added in an effort to salvage the situation. *I have just realised that I have no choice but to kill you because I know that you will eventually hurt me in just the same way my grandfather did.*

"Let me fix you a drink," Stefan smiled. She watched as he went over to the wine rack and uncorked a bottle of red wine. They sat together on the sofa talking and the talk eventually turned to Helena's family. She told Stefan of her parents being killed in the blitz and being brought up by her maternal grandparents. He watched her face and saw the pain etched into her nervous smile as she drifted back in time to the death of her grandparents when she was 14 years of age. She stopped short of telling him the circumstances of the grandparents death only that afterwards, she was left all alone in the world. She told him that she was brought up in an orphanage until she was old enough to take care of herself.

Stefan sat in a stunned, awkward silence not knowing where to look as her tragic story unfolded in pitiful detail. Eventually, when she stopped speaking, he lifted his hand and wiped away the tears running down her face. He felt so sorry for her and he just wanted to take her in his arms to hold her close until the tears eventually ceased. Helena looked deeply into Stefan's eyes and saw that he felt her pain and suffering almost every bit as she did. For several minutes they remained locked in a warm embrace before Helena whispered a faint, "Thank you."

"Thank you for what?" he asked.

"Thank you for listening," she said as she gave him a gentle kiss. They had no control as they looked into each others eyes and the flames of passion were lit once again.

Taking hold of Stefan's hand, Helena led him into her bedroom and, without taking her eyes from his face, began to undress until she eventually stood naked in front of him. She walked tantalisingly toward him and his heart beat so fast he thought it was about to explode. He had never seen such stunning beauty. His whole world seemed to slow into a bizarre scene from some epic silver-screen moment until she finally stood just a matter of inches away from him. She wrapped her arms around his neck and began to kiss him passionately. In wild abandon she began to tear at his clothes and he did not protest and soon they were both naked. Their hands began to feverishly explore each other's bodies and before long they were rolling around the bed enjoying the rampant, animal pleasures of their bodies once again. Even in the throes of such ecstatic delight like some kind of Preying Mantis Helena's mind was focussed firmly on Stefan dying that very night. Her plans were laid and his 'surprise' was waiting to be unleashed.

Two hours later exhaustion descended once again on the frantic lovers. Stefan lit a cigarette as Helena slipped from the bed to take a shower.

"I want to cook for you," she smiled as she emerged from the shower with a towel round her hair.

"Is that my surprise, or is what we just did my surprise?" he joked.

"I told you once that you will never guess, neither of those are your surprise,"

"You mean my surprise will be better that what just happened?" he asked incredulously.

"Oh yes my lover…infinitely better," she smiled.

As they ate, Helena casually turned the talk around to suggest a walk after supper to which Stefan readily agreed. Inside he could have cheerfully given it a miss, but for the sake of romance he would have gone along with anything she suggested. Helena slipped on her long coat and stepped out into the street. Arm in arm the lovers walked in perfect rhythm towards the lights of the town in the distance. Helena mentioned the alley that ends at the beginning and of course Stefan is intrigued by such a strange place. There had been talk of putting street lights in the alley but when they arrived, Helena was pleased to see that this had not yet taken place. Stefan's excitement at finding the alley in darkness was a world away from Helena's; she was excited because she knew beyond any doubt that her evil plan would succeed.

Taking Stefan by the hand, Helena led him into the alley. She walked slowly and made sure she stayed very close to the wall, on and on into the darkness they walked until eventually they had come full circle. Stefan was fascinated by this and he asked if they might walk along it again. *Perfect, he has fallen right into my trap!* Helena knew that on the second time around he had only one thought on his mind...to make love to her in the shadows of the next doorway. He slid his arm around her shoulders as she allowed herself to be guided down the alley and into the darkness. As she walked she began to finger the handle of the knife she had so carefully concealed in her coat. By now the touching of the knife had become almost a ritual. *Soon my baby you will give me the sacrifice to my father.*

Stefan looked into the darkness and saw the perfect place for him to rest in the arms of his girl. In his mind he was rehearsing every move that would lead to such beautiful wickedness, he would soon be making love to Helena right there in the street and he could hardly contain his excitement. "This reminds me of my very first kiss," he whispered, "Do you feel like doing something daring?" he asked expectantly.

"I feel like doing something outrageously dangerous," she smiled. Stefan backed into the darkened doorway and pulled Helena gently towards him. His lips opened in anticipation as she stepped closer to join him. "Unbutton your coat," he sighed slowly. "I want to give you your surprise right now," she cooed.

"Give it to me slowly my lover," he said.

"First you must close your eyes," she said.

The tension built up to a crescendo as all kinds of wild exotic thoughts poured into his brain in anticipation of what she was about to do. He closed his eyes and listened to the rustling of her clothes, he wanted to steal a glimpse of what he knew was her naked body as he pictured her coat being dropped gently to the floor.

"Now open your eyes," she said seductively.

He opened his eyes just long enough for him to see a blade flashing towards his stomach; seconds later it was buried so deep that it had touched his spine. All sense of feeling from the waist down evaporated in that instant. Helena stood back and watched as Stefan fell silently to the ground. The pathetic, childlike expression on his face suddenly brought her momentarily to her senses and she put her hands over her mouth to stifle her cries. She backed out of the doorway and into the alley; she could not stand to watch him die like that. She slumped against the alley wall and began to sob; she waited until she knew he was dead. Taking tentative steps, she walked back to the doorway to where he had fallen. *This can not be!* There was no sign of Stefan's body. Looking around her, in total confusion she strained her eyes into the darkness all around her, *No this isn't possible; I killed him!* Through her tears she noticed several rubbish bins against the alley wall, she ran towards them but she found nothing. She thought he must have tried to crawl away and had fallen down in amongst the rubbish, but it was no use, he simply was not there. Suddenly she heard voices in the distance, they were probably the voices of drunken revellers but she decided not to take the chance, she had to get out of there and fast. On arriving at her front door, Helena fished in her pockets for her keys and discovered she did not have the knife with her. In her confused mixed state of sadness and euphoria she had left the blade embedded in Stefan's abdomen. She became frantic and considered retracing her steps but decided that it would not be wise. Yes her fingerprints might be on the handle but nobody could trace them back to her. Besides, the night was too dark and the moon had gone behind the rain clouds so she would not be able to find it and if she did, she would also find Stefan and that was a thought too horrific to contemplate. She decided the knife would wait until tomorrow when either his body would be found or she would go back and look for it. She closed her door and leaned against it. As she took off her coat she realised that she was crying. At first she could not figure out why, but eventually decided that the tears were for Stefan and their love making. Throwing her wet coat onto the floor, she slowly made her way to bed where she cried herself to sleep. Sleep came easily that night, but...so did the dream.

## Chapter Sixteen

Helena slowly opened her eyes to find herself standing against the wall of the alley. She looked over her right shoulder expecting to see the shadow hovering there, but it was nowhere in sight. It seemed to have vanished. Helena breathed a sign of relief. She was so relieved to be rid of the shadow that had plagued her for so long. As she rested against the wall she felt so incredibly tired, she was utterly exhausted. She opened her heavy eyes wide and looked at the doors in front of her; she noticed that there was something wrong. At first she could not put her finger on it but she eventually realised, there were only four doors. Knowing there would be no escape for her she made a decision, she knew what she must do, but, in that moment of confusion she could not bring herself to choose a door.

She put her hands behind her back to stop herself from involuntarily reaching out before she was clear in her mind which door to open. Once again she rested her weary head against the wall. She was suddenly seized by a torrent of emotion, was it fear or anger? She could not understand its source and thought it must be because she knew what she had done to Stefan was so wrong for so many reasons; whilst at the same time knowing that she had no choice but to end his life. *Get a hold of yourself Helena!* She justified his death once more by the fact that he would have eventually ended up hurting her and she would never go through that experience again. *Better to hurt than be hurt, better to kill than be killed.* She let her tears erupt like streams of molten lava spewing from the bowels of the earth, she wanted to feel each drop as it burned her face, it would be ideal therapy because the tears reminded her of the tears she cried for her dead mother in the cold lonely hours after her grandfather's evil midnight visits. *Tears that taste like this are good.* She looked down at the handkerchief she had automatically taken from her pocket and she folded it neatly again.

Several minutes passed before Helena eventually found the courage and willpower to move away from the wall. With a great deal of effort coupled with hesitancy, she eventually began to move toward the green door. Once again, she looked all around her to see if the shadow had returned, but it was nowhere to be seen. Her heart pounded in her breast as she dared to think that maybe she had seen the last of the shadow. Taking hold of the green door handle, she hesitated before turning the handle. Doubts began to creep in as to whether she should or not. Her hand trembled against the cold steel of the handle as she realised she had no choice in the matter at all; she had to go forward. Tightening her grip on the handle she turned it; a breath of sweet scented air swept past her as she pushed the door open and stepped inside.

A myriad of emotions raced through her brain once she had committed herself to whatever awaited her on the other side of the door. She tentatively looked over her right shoulder and was just in time to see the door close behind her. As before there was no handle on this side of the door, and she sensed that the moment she walked away from the door, it would disappear—and it did. Pulling her stoic gaze away from where the door had been she found herself in a field full of beautiful flowers; it didn't make any sense. Looking all around her she soon discovered there were no buildings near so, she set off to walk along the path that seemed to come from the door and lead to who knows where? After walking for what seemed like hours, she eventually reached the end of the path to find herself in front of another door. Despite the fatigue in her aching limbs she forced her hand slowly towards the handle of the door. As she touched the door, it opened with ease and she found herself back in her own bedroom. How strange it was to be standing by the bed, watching herself sleeping.

She watched as the body on the bed began to twitch and she realised that she was just beginning to awaken. Moments later Helena sat up in bed and rubbed her eyes. She felt very confused and unsure of her surroundings. Staying where she was, she looked all around her but everything was as it should be. For some reason, she suddenly felt very calm and content and the melancholy she had felt lately due to Stefan's death appeared to have been lifted. *Today is going to be a new day and a new beginning.* She threw back the bedclothes and padded into the bathroom to shower. She felt content and relaxed, her night's work was complete and apart from the slight hitch of the missing knife, everything went according to plan. The next crucial part of her plan was to live as normal a life as possible so as not to attract any attention, with that in mind she decided that she would fill her day with nothing but fun.

She remembered seeing a poster on her last trip to town advertising a new fair that had arrived in town so she intended to spend the better part of the whole day sampling the delights of the fairground that she had so longed for as a child. If she had known what was waiting for her at the end of the day… she would have stayed at home.

The fairground with all its multi-coloured booths and attractions was the very first one Helena had ever been to. She was indeed like a child and she had every intention of making up for lost time. She looked on amazed at all the many different things at the fair, merry-go-rounds, hoopla, coconut shies, big dippers, a Helter-Skelter and many other attractions. The fair had turned out to be everything Helena had hoped it would be and she tried everything at least once. She even won a goldfish in a bag on the coconut shy and a huge teddy bear on the rifle shooting; if she had been looking for another victim to butcher she would have had no problem at all judging by the amount of admiring glances she was attracting.

The light was starting to fade in the evening sky and the last of the thrill-seekers were wearily beginning to leave the fairground. It had been an absolutely fantastic day and Helena decided it was time she too went home. She was mindful too of the evening's knife errand she had to deal with. As she filed toward the exit a young child ran in front of her and almost knocked the goldfish bag from her hands as she fell to the ground. The child was admonished by her parents and, with a sheepish look on her face, she apologised to Helena. Helena smiled at the little girl and, helped her to her feet. "No need to apologise, I should have looked where I was going too," she said. It was then that a most chilling and extraordinary thing happened. Helena was about to walk through the gates when she heard a voice calling to her: "Helena, why did you kill me?" the voice boomed. In total shock Helena looked all around her, but there was no-one to be seen. Again the voice called: "Helena, why did you kill me?" Searching the faces of other people leaving the fairground and seeing no reaction she realised that only she could hear the pleading echo. She doubled her step to hurry away but if she had only turned, she would have seen Stefan standing on the opposite pavement watching her...but Stefan was dead, wasn't he?

Once free from the general fairground exodus Helena headed for the sanctuary of her flat. Inside she frantically slammed the door shut behind her. She rammed home the bolts to lock it and turned the key then she stood looking at it while she trembled in fear and rage. Without taking her eyes away from the door she backed away until the backs of her legs touched the sofa. With a look of sheer terror on her face she clutched the teddy bear prize to her chest. Visions of Stefan staring down at her filled her whirling mind and she began to weep uncontrollably.

## Chapter Seventeen

Klaus Bauer sat in his chair opposite Helena, making notes as she calmly recounted what she had done. He watched as her face went from sublime happiness to the depths of despair. He looked at her as she smiled and asked "Why are you smiling Helena?" In her Zombie, trance like state, she answered mechanically: "Because I know it will soon be time for me to kill again."

Klaus had never heard a patient talk quite as candidly as this before, even under hypnosis a patient still has some capacity to choose what information to reveal. Perhaps something in her illness made her unaware of what she was saying? Nevertheless, he looked visibly shocked. He sensed that he was on the verge of some kind of major breakthrough but his session had already gone on longer than the recommended medical time. He knew he should stop the session but what he didn't know was that... Helena knew it too. She had chosen her time to tease him and leave him tantalizingly dangling in the air to perfection. He looked at his watch *Damn it!* "Helena, I am going to count from 10 down to 1 and on the word wake you will wake up and feel refreshed, you will remember nothing of our conversation." With that, he brought her from her *hypnotic* state and she lay on the couch with a look of innocence and serenity on her face.

Time seemed to stand still as Klaus finally put his notebook on his desk. Without moving from his chair, he sat and looked at Helena. He was beginning to wonder where he stood as far as she was concerned. Saying nothing as he observed her he used those minutes to reflect on his position, after all he was a prison psychiatrist, and had been for twenty odd years. Finally, he put his hands together as if in prayer and sat with his hands in front of his face looking at Helena lying before him so peacefully. After a further few minutes he formally ended the session for the day. Klaus watched Helena leaving the room and, as she closed the door behind her, he reached behind him and took from his cupboard a bottle of scotch and a glass. He owed himself a stiff drink after a good day's work, what he didn't realise was that

Helena had played him with the same glorious craftsmanship as a virtuoso would lovingly play a Stradivarius violin.

Several minutes passed before Klaus eventually rose from his chair. He walked to the window with his glass in his hand and stood watching the scene below him. Some days, he felt like a prisoner himself being locked up behind the same walls that confined so many dangerous criminals. *I suppose at the end of the day I can leave this place and go home.* He stood and watched the prisoners in the exercise yard with the armed guards keeping a close eye on them. It was a woman's prison and there were several female officers but the majority of the inmates were class A psychopaths so the bulk of the guards were men and most of them had seen active service in the armed forces. Of all the inmates prisoner 5213706 was the most potentially dangerous; Klaus had been a prison psychiatrist for the better part of twenty years, but never before had a patient of such magnitude been placed in his care. He was beginning to think that just maybe Helena was too far gone in her own little world, a lost cause, when she opened up on that day and gave him a glimmer of hope that he could unfold the evil mysteries of her mind. *Maybe she should be in a mental institution not a prison?* In short, he was beginning to wonder if Helena was either bad or untreatably mad. *She is opening up and I know I can get in there.*

Outside his office Helena was escorted back to her cell and lay on her bed. She could feel the pain in her head returning; sometimes it did after her little mind games with the doctor. The pain however was worth the joy she got from playing with his mind. She knew that the only way to control the pain was to sleep. Sleep however, does not come very easily. As always, the minute she closes her eyes the dream begins again. This time she opens her eyes to find she is still standing in the middle of the field within the green door. She is puzzled and does not understand the meaning of it at all, it has nothing to do with any of her past life, there were never any flowers, just the desolation of bombed out ruins infested with weeds and death and memories of devastation. Finally with a fleeting appearance of the shadow she comes to realise that she will not be finished with the green door until she kills again. She turns to head back toward the door. The moment she reaches it, it disappears. Now she is lost and unsure whether to step further into the field or retrace her steps back to the door. She sits down in the middle of the field to search her mind for the answers. *Show me the direction I must take.*

After a lot of soul searching and an examination of his conscience, Klaus finally decides to continue the sessions with Helena. Her parting shot at the end of their last session had certainly done its work. For him he thought he had come too far along the road to turn back and, for his own peace of mind, he needed to know what happened to the other four victims. *Do I have what it takes to get her back to the place where I had her on the verge of revealing everything?*

The following morning Klaus had Helena brought back to his office, when she entered he felt a sudden rush of adrenalin because of the vulnerable state she was in, he knew he had her exactly where he wanted her, she would be like putty in his hands. Her natural beauty was compromised by her dishevelled appearance, her hair had not been brushed that was obvious. She looked tired, almost hungover and the dark circles round her eyes were a giveaway that she had had little if any sleep at all since their last session. Her look just confirmed that he was nearing his prize…the complete surrender of her mind to his. Helena stopped in the doorway and carefully scanned the room. It looked as though she was checking to make sure there is no-one else in the room. Her dark eyes flit nervously around like a cornered animal. Only when she is finally sure they are totally alone, does she step into the room.

"Close the door," Bauer said in a demanding tone. She was visibly shocked by his command, and dumbly obeyed. His gruff initial approach was part of his plan to unnerve her so that he could offer his sympathy later and so begin the unlocking process.

"Lay down on the couch," he continued in the same tone. He watched her as she makes her way to the couch whilst continuing to look furtively around the room. Once on the couch she waited for his next instruction.

"What are you looking for Helena?" he asks.

She looks up at the ceiling and answers inaudibly.

He presses her again without asking her to repeat herself. "There is no one else here Helena, just you and I. Can you see something or someone else?"

She smiles inwardly knowing that she has put him off balance, her plan has worked like a dream, the hunter has suddenly become the hunted. *He thinks I'm mad…perfect!*

After several more failed attempts to illicit an answer he takes a different tack. He assures her that they are alone in the room and asks if she is feeling settled enough for him to begin the hypnosis, to which she slowly nods her assent.

"Where are you today Helena?" he begins.

*Let me see now, where shall I take the fool?*

"I'm at home in my flat," she replies.

"Tell me what is happening now," he asks eagerly.

Helena starts to tell him what is happening.

"It is a cold morning, the rain is falling and I want to stay in bed, but someone is calling me in the distance."

"Who is calling you Helena?"

*Wouldn't you like to know?* She is enjoying every minute of the session and she is playing him like a game fish.

"I can hear a voice but I can't make it out," she whispers as her face takes on the look of straining to identify the voice.

"Is it male or female?" he presses.

Helena ignores the question and goes off on a tangent, "Stefan stayed with me all through the night last night."

"What happened last night then; describe last night," he says impatiently.

*Now for some fun!*

"I slowly pulled myself out of bed and walked slowly along to the bathroom. While I walk I am thinking of Stefan and the unbelievable passion we have just shared and then I ask myself 'Did he really die? Is he still alive? If so, where is he now? I want to know the answers…I force myself to take a cold shower and I allow the water to trickle from my erect nipples. I feel his breath against them, kissing them, caressing them," she moans.

Bauer can hardly control his excitement as Helena begins to writhe on the couch just inches from his trembling hands. Knowing that he is turned on at her vulnerability she turns the screw a little more before she brings him down to earth with a shuddering thud of an anti-climax. "The water against my skin awakens me and I want him to take me again."

"And does he?" Bauer asks hoping to be given the full explicit details.

"I think I will go shopping today," she says.

"Shopping?" Bauer almost shouts in exasperation at another sudden change in direction.

*Down boy!*
"I am afraid that I will see Stefan again. I must decide if I should stay indoors or venture out. I try to put everything into perspective and finally decide that I will go out; after all I have to find my next victim…he won't come running to me…will he?
"But what about Stefan? Listen to my voice Helena, listen only to my voice. Let me take you back to the bedroom with Stefan," he says in a voice bordering on pleading.

*Oh you naughty doctor, isn't there a law against professional misconduct?*

She teases him mercilessly, "Ghosts only come out after dark, don't they?" she asks.

"Ghosts? shopping? Helena, where are you going?"

"Stefan is dead and the dead don't always return do they?"

"No Helena, the dead don't return," he says dejectedly. He knows that with her obvious state of mind that this session is going nowhere fast.

"I am going to count from 10 to 1 and when you wake…"

# Chapter Eighteen

Helena stood outside her gate with her back resting on the metal fence. She looked all around her and wherever she looked, it seemed that the streets were deserted. Helena tried hard to focus her attention on just what is ahead of her. She thought that if she tried not to look around, she would be safe, but safe from what or who she was not sure of. She no longer felt safe on the streets and she began to wonder if she should quit whilst she was ahead and stop the killings. It was her first sane thought in weeks; sane as in there was no conflicting voice in her head telling her to kill relentlessly and without mercy. She kept on walking without realising that she had entered the park. She approached a bench and cautiously sat down to think things through. She was so deep in thought that she even failed to notice the man sitting opposite her. He sat staring straight at her for several minutes before Helena eventually raised her head and caught him looking at her.

At first she was startled and a little bemused, firstly she thought she was alone but secondly she thought his face was familiar but she couldn't place him straight away. She was convinced that she had met this man before, but try as she might she has no idea where from. *Perhaps he looks like Stefan. No, that isn't it.* Without taking her eyes off the young man, she got up from the bench and began to walk away from him. He let her walk so far ahead of him knowing that she would turn around to see if he was following her. He knew that his eye contact had done enough to ignite her interest. He was right; as she neared the end of the path leaving the park she turned her head just enough to let him see that there was an opportunity to develop if he wanted to take it. She saw that he was still on the bench but he was watching her every move. He was not following her, but as she continued to walk away she knew that it would be just a matter of moments before their eyes would meet again on some pretext or another. She left the park and headed towards home. By the time she had reached the point in the road where she wanted to cross he was already in her slipstream. She smiled inwardly at her prediction and at his *male on the make* predictability. Suddenly she was gripped by a sensation that unnerved her, it was a kind of fear that was new to her and she didn't like it one bit. She stole a furtive look over her shoulder and saw the young man just a few yards away from her. Something told her that it would be unwise to go home, there was something different about this man; she needed another good look at him to see if his clothes might give away his motives for being there but she was too afraid to take another look. *I don't want him to know where I live, he feels like trouble.*

She crossed the road dodging in and out of traffic, to the consternation of one or two irate drivers. On the far side she looked back and saw that for the time being the young man had gone. She breathed a sigh of relief as she scanned the immediate vicinity to see where he might have gone. Did she imagine she was being followed? She was sure he was behind her only moments earlier so where had he gone? Half of her wanted to run as fast as she could anywhere that would take her away from that place; but the other half, the more stoical half, told her to take the long way back to her flat to make sure that he was indeed gone. Darkness was beginning to fall and she would rather not be out and feeling vulnerable in the growing gloom. Paranoia kicked in as a form of protection; *He may be watching me from the shadows...if he is, I will make him regret it!*

Sitting in the relative safety and comfort of her own home, Helena knew that she had to analyse her sudden fear of the dark, it just didn't make any sense. Never in all of her life has she been scared of whatever the night brings, even when her torture was at its most horrendous as a child, she had always welcomed the darkness as a comforting friend. *I still have so much work to do, work that cannot be done in the daylight hours.* The silence of the night is the right time for her. The coal black stillness of a moonless night is the place she has always loved, so why the sudden fear? She decided that over the course of the next few days she must force herself to go out into the night and stay out a little longer each time, that way maybe she will get her nerve back. The thoughts of that resolution brought her some assurance, but that resolution was hanging by a thread. It would have snapped immediately if she had seen the stranger lurking in the shadows, watching her flat from across the road.

The night had turned dark and an oppressive, stale feeling lingers in the air about her, the chill told her that it was about to rain. She walked to the window and looked out into the darkness. As she watched the black, billowing clouds overhead the rain began to fall in a fragmented rhythm dictated by the ever changing swirling of the wind. *Why does it always seems to be raining? Maybe the sun will begin to shine soon?* Closing the curtains she turned and switched on the small table lamps at either side of the sofa; they cast a warm and cosy light around the room. The rain falling steadily heavier against the windows made the thought of a long hot soak in the bath feel like the most luxurious gift to herself that she could think of. Perhaps the heat of a scented bath would calm her body and bring on a restful sleep? She walked through into the bathroom and turned on the hot tap. She let it flow through her fingers until the initial warmth turned to blistering hot. As the bath began to fill, she went back into the lounge and mindlessly turned on the television. It was a musical documentary about the romantic musicians of the nineteenth century.

*Ah how timely, a hot bath and music made for lovers, what a beautiful way to relax, one that Stefan would approve of.* With her body fully submerged and the heat of the water turning her muscles to wax she realised how tense she had become lately. She made a resolution, *tomorrow, I will begin looking for my third victim, I cannot allow the image of my beloved Stefan to change my only course of action.*

Helena slept peacefully that night; the bath had done its job. It was the first time in a long time that no dreams had invaded her mind. She could not remember the last time she had such a peaceful night; it was exactly what she needed.

She awoke the next morning totally refreshed and ready for a new day and ready to face the world. Helena promised herself that today was going to be a good day. She planned to stay home all day and catch up on her studies which she had been neglecting of late and, as dusk was falling she would venture out for a walk as the first part of her self diagnosed therapy. At first she would probably just take a walk round the block to get back into the habit of going out after dark. She was unsure at first how to cope with this sudden fear of the dark or indeed if her therapy was the right course of action. One thing was for certain and that was that she had to find the Helena of old, the girl who thrived on darkness. The only way forward was to face her demons, whatever and whoever they may be.

By 7pm the day was slowly fading into twilight, Helena looked out of her window to see the rain was also beginning to fall. She stood almost transfixed, looking out at the rain for some time before deciding it was nothing more than a shower, a short walk round the block wouldn't get her too wet. Pulling on her boots and hooded coat she picked up her keys and went out of the front door taking great care to lock it behind her. She hesitated on the doorstep before venturing any further. She called on all her senses to alert her to any danger before she took one more step. Only when she was satisfied that her straining ears would have picked up any strange sounds did she take that first step. The moment her foot touched the pavement beyond the boundaries of her home her body shuddered as if she has been struck by a bolt of lightning and she stood rooted to the spot. Standing not two steps in front of her was the same young man from the park. For the first time in years she did not know what to do, her heart was pounding in her chest like a hammer on a cold anvil. There was a time when she was fearless, impervious to anything the world could hurl at her but...this young man frightened her. From the back, he looked so much like Stefan. The initial shock of seeing him turned quickly into panic and despite her mind giving instructions to her legs she remained unable to move for the life in her. Part of her was screaming at her to go back inside, but another voice was telling her to simply walk in the other direction until he was hers for the killing.

After that mental struggle within she went with the second voice and to hell with it...but... *Who is he?*

As she walked, she looked over her shoulder trying not to bring attention to herself whilst at the same time trying to discern his features to put a definite name to them. The first voice in her mind spoke again and told her that she should not be out tonight. The overpowering second voice hissed in her brain that she must carry on, she had plans to make and she knew that if the third kill was not completed soon, the dream would be back with a vengeance. She knew that the dream would be back anyway, but perhaps not with the same ferocity and if she was able to figure out what she must do each time the dream recurred, at least the shadow would be kept at bay. She hated the dreams, but she hated the shadow even more because she was certain that it was the reincarnation of her evil grandmother.

All manner of thoughts flew through Helena's mind as she walked aimlessly in a semi-conscious daze through street after street until finally she realised she was in the centre of town. The town was eerily quiet except for a dog barking in the distance. The short walk she had promised herself had driven her way further away from home than she wanted to be...*who was that young man who forced me away from my home?* It was time to stop walking and take a look at the rapidly worsening situation that was closing in on her like claustrophobia. Looking all around her she saw nothing but the deserted rain sodden streets. Suddenly she heard the sound of footsteps...*No; get a hold of yourself Helena that is a fox scavenging for scraps of food...not footsteps.* She cautiously walked towards the sound and as she peered around the corner she was just in time to witness the young man disappearing around the far corner of the street and out of her sight. *Enough is enough I am going to see where he has gone.* She did not like the feeling of being hunted, especially by someone who appeared to know the state of her mind and the frailty of her tangled emotions. *This man is beginning to worry me.*

With her mind still in turmoil and confusion she stood looking at the spot where he had disappeared. Undaunted she summoned an inner strength from deep within her being and steeled herself to do what had to be done. She walked the full length of the street to the far corner, only to find he had totally disappeared. *This is impossible!* There were no corners he could hide around, no shop doorways he could use for shelter. It was as if he had vanished into thin air. Was he real or was he just a figment of Helena's imagination? She no longer knew what to believe, one thing was certain, if she ever saw this young man again…and he was for real… he would be victim number three.

## Chapter Nineteen

Helena walked home puzzling over whom this young man was; why was he following her? What did he want? By now, the earlier light rain was falling heavier and the overcast sky looked dark and foreboding. Suddenly there was an almighty deluge and Helena was soaked through to the skin. It was evident that the stormy weather was not going to let up for the rest of the night and, by the time she arrived at her own front door, Helena had had just about all she could take for one day. Taking off her coat and boots she half slid, half walked into the flat. She hung her saturated coat on the hook at the back of the door and carried her soaking wet boots into the bathroom to dry out. Whilst in the bathroom, she stripped off all her clothing and put them into the laundry basket ready for washing. She climbed mechanically into the shower cubicle and looked at her distorted reflection in the mirror opposite. *Is this the sum total of my life, one long distorted view? Is this how the world sees me and if not, why not? This is who I am, a distorted reflection of who I am supposed to be.*

She let the hot water burn into her reddening skin as she closed her eyes to try and picture something wild and beautiful that would replace her troubled memories of childhood torment. The pain of the water might purge her soul of all the terrible things she had done and would yet do. She murmured a brief prayer of forgiveness and as it evaporated toward heaven with the rising steam so the day's worries washed away in the vortex in the floor of the shower.

It seemed like an eternity before she eventually opened her eyes to feel herself totally relaxed and at ease for the first time in years. The flowing water had not only cleansed her body, it appeared to have cleansed her mind and her soul too. *Perhaps my prayer reached the forgiver of wicked sins?* Once more she was revitalised and she felt ready to face the world and whatever it flung at her. Stepping out of the shower she put on her slippers and wrapped her bathrobe around her wallowing in the luxurious comfort of the softness of it. She was determined not to let any negative thoughts invade her settled mind; she owed it to herself to have at least one night of pleasant enjoyment; even if that meant doing absolutely nothing. She turned on the television and curled up on the sofa. From where she sat she could see out of the window and she was pleased to see that the rain had finally stopped. Although it was early evening, it was quite dark outside and Helena had to put on the table lamps. She went to the window and drew the heavy drapes. As she shut out the world there was an immediate feeling of warmth and cosiness in the room but, most of all, Helena felt safe. Like a diligent prison guard locking up for the night she went through her ritual of checking all the windows and closing all the curtains in each room. Once she was satisfied that her own little world felt secure she flopped onto the sofa to watch the latest news. She had not been seated more than a few moments when she thought about checking the bedroom. She tried to convince herself that the bedroom had not been touched since she left it secure earlier in the day. It was no use; the niggling thoughts persisted so she dragged herself wearily to her feet. She opened the bedroom door and immediately knew that there was something not quite right...the bedroom window was wide open. As far as she could remember, she could not recall having opened any windows due to the bad weather. She stood in the bedroom doorway and looked all around as far as she could to make sure there was no-one in the room. Eventually, her eyes were drawn back to the open window. The feeling that some-one had been in the flat gripped her heart. *Anyone could have walked in on me at any time at all; maybe there is still someone in here?*

She was suddenly overcome by a feeling of intense terror. She had no choice but to force herself over to close the window and curtains. Unnerved she once again went through every room in the flat and searched everywhere just to satisfy herself that there was no-one else on the premises. Now that she was sure she was on her own she bolted the front door and locked it with the key. *Perhaps now I can finally relax a little.* The fatigue that had invaded her body after she had killed Stefan came back with a vengeance and demanded interest and within just a few minutes she fell asleep.

Not one hour had past before she woke up with a jolt. As she looked fleetingly around the room she suddenly felt aware that someone was watching her. She closed her eyes and instead of relying on her sight she intensified her sense of hearing and listened for the sounds of someone moving around; but not a sound was to be heard. As she was about to open her eyes she heard a sound that made her blood run cold...something was scratching from inside the cavity of the walls; the more she listened, the more she realised that it was...a rat! Without even bothering to analyse the information flashing from her sense of hearing to her brain, she let out a blood-curdling scream. *Anything but rats!* If she had been less focussed on the rats she might have noticed earlier that standing beside her, watching her every move, was...Stefan.

Scrambling up into the corner of the sofa she could not take her eyes away from the apparition in front of her. Blustering she stammered: "You are dead Stefan. How can you return? Go back to the place I sent you and leave me alone." With tears, a mixture of fear and emotion blinding her disbelieving eyes she looked at the unmistakable form of the man she had loved enough to kill before he could hurt her. "I want to know why you killed me," he said in a voice that sounded detached from the spectre and echoed round the room. She covered her ears to block out the sound but it was no use, the voice was in her head! Again the spirit asked for an answer as it appeared to move towards her menacingly. She cowered away and buried her face in the cushions, "Get away from me!" she screamed again as an ice cold, mist like wave passed over her. The voice began to fade and finally subsided. The seconds seemed like hours as the silence descended on the room. With terror and madness in her eyes they darted round the room but the spirit had gone, disappeared into the silence of the night. *My God, what is happening to me? Was it Stefan or was it all in my mind? Perhaps he is the spectre of too much lost sleep and nothing more?*

It made no difference how much Helena tried to convince herself she was having illusions, no matter how much she tried, she could not settle down for the rest of the night and sat with the cushion clutched closely into her shaking body. The clock on the wall boomed out with each ticking movement of the minute hand. Eventually she nodded off into a restless sleep.

The night seemed to pass in a whirl for Helena. Before she knew it, morning had arrived and she had never been so relieved to see the first rays of daylight ripping through the cold morning like great beams of redeeming energy. She lay motionless for several minutes gathering her thoughts about the night that had just passed before finally letting go of the cushion and sitting upright. She took a cautious look around the room and, only when she was satisfied that all was well, did she venture through into the kitchen.

She felt compelled to exorcise the memory of the apparition which had so painfully invaded her life the night before and she went through each room of the flat. Not knowing what to expect and at the same time expecting anything she felt suddenly courageous in the bright light of the morning. *Where are you now Stefan?* She checked every room before ripping the curtains apart to allow the sunshine to stream in. The sun obligingly filled the rooms with light and lifted Helena's soul. By the time she had opened all the curtains she was convinced that his ghost was nothing more than her imagination. *Perhaps Stefan was telling me that he needs the company of another? Yes of course! He is lonely and longs for a companion to share his darkness. Then you won't have to wait another night my love, I will send you a friend before the night returns.* In her deranged state she stumbled back through to the living room to plan her next move. She was determined that today and no matter what the circumstances, the third victim would die.

There was no time to lose; as twilight descended, Helena went out of the flat to begin her night's work. As she slipped out into the early morning there was no indication to the commuters and passers by that within the right hand pocket of the coat she was wearing this beautiful young woman had a kitchen knife with a four inch blade and cold-blooded murder in her mind. The sun was already warming the overnight dewfall and thin wisps of evaporation snaked skywards. She was surprised by the number of people already out and about, but then again it was a weekday so most of them were workers on their way to start the early shift. Helena listened mechanically to the hum of conversations flitting about in the air until she heard one woman announce that rain was forecast by early evening. *Perfect!* It meant the rain water would wash all the blood away...and there would be no evidence left behind. She no longer cared if the man was young or old but someone was going to die that night. She made her way back to the flat and waited for the weather to break.

# Chapter Twenty

The wind suddenly began blowing quite fiercely and was quickly followed by the rain and, although it was still early in the afternoon, the sunny sky of minutes earlier had become eerily dark. Helena looked out of the window and smiled in satisfaction; the dark foreboding held in the rain clouds underpinned her feeling of bloody success and she shook with wild, murderous anticipation. She pulled on her boots and hooded coat and opened her front door. No one in their right mind would venture out into an impending storm like that but Helena was far from that condition...she had business to conduct!

Helena stood in her open doorway and watched the falling rain for several minutes as it formed into tiny rivulets which in-turn joined tributaries flowing to the gutter before finally swirling into the vortex of the sewer. She stood mesmerised as the excitement began to build in the pit of her stomach. She began to imagine that the rain water was blood splashing over the walls and down the drain. The urgency of the waiting deed began to drag her from her sordid daydream and after several minutes she pulled herself together and ventured out into the snarling teeth of the gathering storm. Closing the door behind her she pulled her hood over her head and began walking in the direction of the town centre. Once again she was careful to fully conceal the wicked blade she carried. Turning her collar to the howling wind she lowered her head down against the driving rain that lashed viciously at her face. She ignored the transitory discomfort; it would be worth it. The death of the third man, whoever it might be, would be adequate compensation a thousand times over.

When the rain is pouring down and winds are howling around there are very few people who venture out in it. Helena found that wherever she walked, whenever she turned a corner, there was not a person in sight. It was not the weather for man or beast to be abroad. She had walked at least half a mile before she encountered anyone at all, and that was a lone woman hurrying home to the comfort of a welcoming house. Another half a mile was gone before she saw ahead of her a man. From a distance, his demeanour was that of a stooping, older man but in the driving rain it was difficult to tell. Not that it mattered at all; his fate was sealed the moment she set eyes on him. Helena fingered the knife held in her right hand coat pocket and was preparing to draw it at the right moment as he approached...*just a few more steps.* Suddenly he ducked into a concealed alleyway and by the time Helena realised where he had gone she saw him again just long enough to see him going into the light from the door he had just opened...*Damn!* She let the knife slip back down deep into her pocket. *Would it be third time lucky?*

She stood in the rain disappointed that her kill had managed to escape until she was soaked right through to the skin. *Perhaps tonight is not going to be the night?* Apart from those two people she had not seen another soul in the two hours she had been out stalking for prey. Dejectedly she decided to return home and wait for another day. She passed several shops with no signs of any customers, even the beer kellers that were usually filled with rowdy revellers looked more like the saloons of western ghost towns. The walk back home was a long and lonely one. Her head forced down by the wind which still showed no sign of relenting and the rain was still falling hard. Her hand involuntarily wrapped around the handle of the knife almost in some strange form of solace, yes, it was a shame she was not going to get the chance to use it, but, it would make the next kill all the sweeter...*he will pay for this delay with the slow delay of his own death.*

She was almost a mile from home when she saw the lights from a café ahead of her. She was cold and wet and a hot drink would go some way towards compensating her. At least the night would not have been a total disaster. She walked into the café and, since there were no customers, she had the choice of where she could sit. She chose a seat away from the window so she could watch in the vain hope that the rain would ease a little before she left. A waitress came to her and took her order almost immediately. "Black coffee!" was Helena's curt response to the young waitress' polite enquiry. The coffee arrived and Helena wrapped her hands around the cup as she lifted it to her lips; her mind drifting off into the desolation of the night outside. A feeling of calm began to run through her as the coffee did its job and warmed her. The rain eased and slowly stopped just as Helena put the cup down for the last time. Then, as she prepared to leave she noticed a glimmer of hope as a man entered the café and brushed past her table. Helena's heart began to race as the man sat down at the table nearby and called out his order, he too wanted only coffee which meant that he would soon be leaving. After he placed his order he looked around the café and saw that he was not alone. He uttered an apology for ignoring her when he entered the café. Helena simply smiled before turning up her collar and stepping out into the street. Instead of heading home she turned left and walked along the road to find a place from which she could keep an eye on the door of the café. She slid into a shop doorway and waited...

Half an hour went by and still the man had not left the café. She glanced at her watch and saw that it was nearing closing time. He would leave the café at any moment, of that she was certain. Sure enough, as the clock chimed round to the hour the man appeared in the doorway of the café and pulled on his gloves as he looked up at the rain clouds once again gathered in the sky. Shaking his head, he turned right and began walking in the opposite direction to Helena.

*Damn!* Helena knew that this would be the last opportunity she would have that night and she was not about to let it pass. She walked quickly and stealthily along the pavement behind the man making sure not to make a sound. He stopped briefly to check for traffic at the edge of the usually busy road and suddenly...he felt a sharp pain in his lower back that took his breath away. He staggered forward before he looked around, it had been just an instant but there was no-one in sight. He did not see the young woman that had stepped from the shadows to deliver the death strike with lightening accuracy. Helena stood in the blacked out shop doorway watching him.

The poor man did not fall down immediately and Helena had to stifle a cry. She was beginning to think that maybe she had not stabbed the knife into his back hard enough and that she would have to come out of hiding. Eventually, the blood flooding into his stomach from his ruptured spleen began to gargle in his throat before he fell onto his knees and finally onto the ground lying with his face on the street. She waited for several minutes before she walked quietly to his side to look at him. A demonic smile flashed across her face as she stood watching the life blood of this unknown man spill onto the old granite cobbles. Looking around her, she saw a rat emerge from the drain and sniff the air as if it had identified the smell of fresh blood as a potential meal. After a high pitched squeal it was joined by others and soon there was an army of the fetid beasts eyeing up the stiffening corpse. As she melted back into the shadows Helena thought she heard his feeble cry for help, she ignored it. *Save your breath to beg the rats to make your end come soon.*

The exhilaration she felt when she finally put the blood-stained knife back into her pocket was immense. She stood still for a minute or two listening to the man pleading for help amongst the sickening squeals of the ravenous rats, then, hearing no more, she began the walk home. The rain had begun to fall again and, although she was by now soaked through, Helena took the long way home. She wanted this feeling of utter supremacy to last as long as possible. She walked into her flat with a smile of exhilaration on her face; *that is it, number three has died.*

The hot shower she took only added to the thrill of the night and, as she let the water take its course, she let her hands roam over her body once again and the strength of her orgasm pulsated through her body like an electric shock. She flopped exhausted onto the bed and soon she was asleep. The dream began again but this time with a difference. Helena opened her eyes to see that she was standing against a wall and in front of her, three doors remained. She was used to this by now, no longer was she afraid because she knew what to expect…or so she thought…

# Chapter Twenty One

Facing Helena were three remaining doors, white, yellow and blue. She was not at all sure what she should do now so, she stood with her back against the wall, wrapped her arms around herself and stared at the doors for some inspired guidance, she was almost like a child trying to choose a favourite toy. She looked from one door to the next and back again finally shaking her head, she had no idea which one to choose. Without knowing why she began to cry and she used the sleeve of her jumper to try and wipe the tears away without success. The more she tried to stem the flow the more they came in a constant stream. Eventually, she gave up and raised her head to find that the yellow door stood open. She paused and looked at the open door through the haze of her misty eyes, she could hardly believe that the choice had been made for her; it was as if it was by magic.

She dared not move at first, she did not know why the door had opened for her. She knew that she would have to make a move soon so she stirred from the wall and steeled herself ready for what she had to do. Moving toward it and, before entering it, she looked around to see if the shadow that usually plagued her dreams was following her, it wasn't. At least now she was able to breathe a sigh of relief. She thought that all she had to do now was walk through that door and face whatever it was waiting for her on the other side; she then had to work out how to deal with it and get back to the business of death. Still she hesitated and stood just on the threshold of the doorway looking around at everything in front of her. Inside the yellow door there stood a house. It was painted white and it looked as if it had a lot of rooms, but somehow it did not seem to take up a lot of space...*is it a doll's house?* Helena stepped over the threshold never taking her eyes off the house until she heard the door close behind her. Without looking round, Helena knew that all she could do now was to go forward... as always, there was no going back.

Klaus could only look on as Helena lay on the sofa with the tears running down her face. He asked her gently: "Helena, why are you crying?" "Can you see these tears?" She asked as her hand automatically reached up to wipe them away.

"Yes Helena, I see them, what makes you cry so?"

"I don't know," she sobbed, "I don't want to talk just now, I need to see what I am doing."

"What do you need to see, Helena?" Klaus asked quietly. He asked her to describe what was happening to her.

"I see a house with many rooms," she said.

"Tell me more about the house," he urged.

"You have to leave me alone so that I can see for myself," Helena said in a voice that really was trying to fathom something out.

"Take your time Helena and tell me everything so that I can help you," Klaus said as he feverishly scribbled in his notebook.

With Klaus's carefully worded questions probing her, Helena sounded like a robot as she slowly thought out what was before her eyes before answering all the questions he put to her. She stopped many times halfway through the answers and Klaus had to ask her repeatedly to continue. He was fully aware of the emotions she was going through but that had nothing to do with his brief which was to find out if the woman before him was sane or insane. He could see every pain etched into her young and pretty face as her story of what was in the room unfolded. He began to feel sorry for her but there was nothing he could do to help her; his job was to listen and analyse and that is what he would do.

Klaus sat at a distance from her at first as regulations stipulated but her voice was fluctuating in tone and resonance so much that he had no choice but to get up and walk over to her. He stood at a relatively comfortable distance looking down at her and he could see her face tortured and twisted with pain one minute then smiling the next. He needed to work out what she was thinking of as she smiled, he felt that the smile was the crux of everything; he needed to identify a pattern. He shook his head as he watched because he could see she was recalling events from her distant past. Five minutes later, he walked back to his chair and sat down with a heavy heart. The young woman in front of him was beginning to worry him. Many times in the past few weeks, he had gone home with the weight of the world on his shoulders wondering what he could and should do to help her. A conclusion began to form in his mind, but was it a conclusion that benefitted him or the woman he was supposed to be treating?

Klaus sat in his chair with his hands held together in front of him as if in prayer. Helena had grown silent so he took the opportunity to reflect. After several quiet moments he slowly brought Helena out of her trance and ended the session for the day. At first, when she awoke, she did not understand where she was. Klaus did something that was totally unorthodox; he took hold of her by the shoulders and led her towards the door. He opened the door for her and, as she walked along the corridor back to her cell, he stood in the doorway looking at her retreating back. Helena got back to her cell in a daze. She really had no idea where she was and how she had got here.

As she sat on the edge of her bed, her mind began to wander back to the days when she had lived her own life in her own little world with no stress and no confusion, a world where she had everything she needed…except for the love of family. Now, she sat in the silence of her cell with four bare walls, no books, no radio and no company. She was utterly alone and finally the horror of what she had accomplished began to dawn on her.

Helena slowly edged her way onto the bed until her back was against the hard brick wall. She had no shoes on her feet because they had been taken away when she was brought into prison. A simple pair of slippers stood on the floor next to her bed. Her only possession, a picture of her cat, stood on the little table by the bed accompanied by a plastic jug full of water and a plastic cup. *My God, is this the culmination of my life?*

She sat on the bed looking all around her and the silent tears welled up again from their pitiful slumber. This time the tears were for her and she understood why. All of her life so far had been built on hatred and the need to kill to be happy. She finally realised this was all wrong, she had never been happy, apart from the time she spent with Stefan. Seeing his face in her mind's eye, she let the tears have full vent and, eventually she cried herself to sleep. Across town in a bedroom filled with books and CD's and all the trappings of success, Klaus read over his scribbled notes and he wondered which one of them was really in prison.

The following morning, she was woken by the guard and taken to the canteen where the guard stood and watched as Helena sat and ate her breakfast alone. She was allowed no contact with any of the other prisoners. Only now did Helena realise the horrendous enormity of her actions and began to feel remorse for the things she had done…or did she?

Two hours later, Helena was sitting on the edge of the couch in Klaus's room. He could see she was struggling to tell him something but she did not know where to begin. Gently he prompted her from the notes he had made the day before and she began to open up to him, albeit, painfully slowly. She started by telling him of the recurring nightmare she had every night for the past three years. She had no way of knowing that everything she was saying, Klaus already knew about. He listened very patiently without speaking while Helena spoke, pausing, but uninterrupted. She could not bring herself to look at Klaus as she spoke, choosing instead to stare at a mark on the wall ahead of her. She began by telling him of the never ending alley, the dream of the rats, the shadow following her along the wall and the different coloured doors that would not disappear until she had completed a kill. Time passed slowly for Helena and at last she fell silent. It seemed that she had been talking for hours and Klaus could see the exhaustion in her face as she brought her semi-soliloquy to a close. In all the time he had spent with her, Klaus had never heard her reveal so much and so willingly.

Klaus sat silently for a few minutes appearing to assimilate everything Helena had said. Finally, he moved his chair closer to the couch where Helena sat. She had remained still throughout the whole session with her hands clasped together looking down at the floor. Slowly, she raised her head and looked at Klaus. There appeared to be no emotion or judgment on his face but she knew he had listened to her every word. She knew she needed help and this was the only chance she was going to get, it would come from his recommendation alone and nothing else. *Have I done enough?*

Klaus said nothing; he waited instead for Helena to speak again. After a little while, she said in an almost imperceptible voice: "Please help me. I can't do this on my own anymore. I need help." At last, the words Klaus had been waiting to hear had been said. Taking Helena's hands in his own, he said: "Of course I will help you Helena. That's what I'm here for. Now your treatment can begin. Would you like that?" She smiled weakly and Klaus could almost feel the release of pressure lifting from her weary shoulders.

# Chapter Twenty Two

Now that Helena had finally asked for his help all of Klaus's training told him that the time was right to begin the treatment that she would need to bring her back into the world of sanity. He spoke to her as if he had never used this method before, and told her that the first thing he would do would be to place her in a hypnotic trance.

"Yes I know," she said in a submissive voice, "I've been in a trance before. What will change this time to make anything different?"

"This time Helena, I am taking you back to when you were a child and will lead you through all your childhood years up to the present day. By doing this we should be able to find the reasons behind your...your problems. Is that ok with you?" He was careful not to mention the heinous crimes she had committed.

Helena listened as his words seemed to hang in the air around her. After several moments she slowly nodded her assent. She had no way of knowing that Klaus already had most of the answers to things that had been tormenting her so, in her mind everything he was about to do was new. That was what she would have to make him believe at any rate, and as his voice dropped a full tone into his hypnotic voice, Helena smiled inwardly, he had sniffed at the bait and was about to swallow it in spectacular fashion.

In accordance with procedure Klaus made sure that Helena was comfortable with what he was about to do and that she was happy to proceed. She lay down on the couch and waited for Klaus to begin. Still he hesitated and Helena could sense a build up of tension. She was certain that it did not originate from her so she kept her cool and allowed things to unfold at his pace. He had still not begun after five minutes so Helena opened her eyes and asked why he was waiting.

"I need to be a hundred percent certain that this will be the right thing for you, I want my preparations to be perfect. You just close your eyes and relax and I will be ready presently."

*He hasn't got a clue what he is doing!* Helena thought. In fact, he was gathering the notes he had already made to see if there would be any difference in what she told him willingly this time. After another agonising pause he was ready and the hypnosis began. Helena listened to the droning of his voice and waited just long enough to look as though she was completely hypnotised and transported back in time to the brick wall, in front of which were only three doors. Suddenly Helena was seized by an attack of panic and self doubt. *Am I under hypnosis or am I still awake?* The familiar doors appeared in her mind and she was overcome by an intense feeling of exhaustion. She could hear his voice in the distance but still she could not decide what was really going on. *Perhaps he is smarter than he looks?* She decided to go with the flow and see what developed.

She was not the least bit afraid of what was behind the doors. Once again, the yellow door stood open and once again Helena walked through it into the garden where the white house stood. The door closed behind her but this time she was ready to see whatever was in the house and whatever waited around every corner.

Cautiously she walked toward the house with a furtive look behind her every step of the way. She had expected to see the shadow behind her but thankfully, there was no sign of it at all. There was a correlation appearing in her mind about when she saw it and when she didn't but she could not solve the enigma. After walking all around the outside of the house, she opened the front door, walked inside and quietly closed the door behind her. With her back against the door, Helena looked around the downstairs of the house. In the centre of the room was a huge staircase at the top of which were corridors leading off to the left and the right. Without moving from the door, she let her eyes wander all around the upstairs of the house finally coming to rest at the foot of the staircase. A mirror image of the upstairs, the ground floor showed doors to the left and the right of her, but Helena ignored these doors. It seemed that a compelling force was encouraging her to go up the staircase. This house felt strange, it seemed that she knew what was behind every door but one, but she couldn't know, she had never been here before…had she?

Steeling herself, she began to walk the few yards to the foot of the staircase. Great beads of perspiration began to run down her face as she slowly ascended the stone staircase. There were two banisters, which Helena held onto for fear of falling. As she walked up the stairs, she occasionally looked behind her expecting to see someone or something following her, but she reached the top of the stairs without incident. When she reached the top of the stairs, she stood still for a few seconds considering which way to go. To the left and right of her were two doors on each side of the banisters, all painted white and all with the same door handles, still Helena was drawn to one particular door. Without taking her eyes away from the door, she turned right and followed the corridor along the landing until she stood outside the furthest door.

This door fascinated her so much, but the thought of what was on the other side scared her to death. Although she still hesitated, she knew she had no choice but to enter. Tentatively, she turned the handle and peered into the darkness of the room. A blast of ice-cold air blew into her face as she stood in the doorway. She closed her eyes and drew a deep breath as she walked into the room and closed the door behind her. She stood facing the door for a minute until she became accustomed to the thin slither of light which appeared to be emanating from the far wall. Slowly turning round she saw in the room a single chair and, sitting in that chair was her grandmother. She stood still as her body froze and she looked open mouthed at her grandmother. There was a smirk on the old woman's face that cut deep into Helena's soul.

"How can this be you? You are dead, I killed you," Helena gasped. The smile remained etched on the old woman's face and she got up from the chair and began walking toward Helena. Helena screamed and instantly the spectre of the old woman vanished into thin air.

Helena lay on the couch in Klaus's office and screamed again in her hypnotic state. Although no sound actually left her mouth, Klaus's instincts were such that he heard the scream and instantly ran to her side. It took him several minutes to calm her down and bring her back to the world of reality. She lay on the couch and her eyes remained closed, afraid to open them, afraid of what she might see. Klaus quietly spoke to her: "Open your eyes Helena. You are safe now. There is no-one to hurt you here." At first she did not respond but after a further prompting she opened her eyes and frantically looked around the room to ensure she was not alone and her grandmother was just in her imagination. She was afraid to ask the question, but she needed an answer, instead Klaus answered it for her. He told her she had been screaming and shouting and he had to bring her back because he felt it was unsafe to carry on. He waited until some semblance of calm returned to her frightened eyes before he asked if she could tell him what had happened.

Slowly she told him that she could remember everything and, hesitantly, Helena began to recall in detail everything that had happened. Klaus sat in muted silence and listened patiently as her story unfolded. He had no need to take notes as he had done that while she was under hypnosis. Klaus's feelings toward Helena were changing in accordance with his changing of his beliefs that she was guilty of anything but child abuse and that the real killers of her victims were her dead grandparents. For the time being, the only thing he wanted was for her to remember what had happened. Only when she had done that, would she begin to recover...and her recovery could be the catalyst for other possibilities.

Klaus tried hard to persuade Helena that it was too risky for her to go back to the house under hypnosis, but Helena was stubborn. She had to know what her grandmother wanted from her. Klaus argued that her grandmother may not even be there anymore, as in Helena's dream, she may have vanished, but Helena would not be dissuaded. She suspected that whatever her grandmother wanted from her would not be good. She had never shown her any love while she had been on this earth, so why would she be any different now? If anything, her return combined with her hatred for humanity in general would make her even more grotesque. Helena was afraid and very nervous, but she also needed closure and answers to questions that she had been afraid to ask when she was a child. Maybe now she had found a path that could lead to her finding out. Klaus knew she was not going to be denied this chance, but he had to do what he could both as a doctor and as one of her jailers. He asked if she was ready to go back and Helena nodded.

# Chapter Twenty Three

Several minutes later, Helena was back in the house, standing in the same room and looking at the same chair. Her blood ran cold when she saw that her grandmother was sitting in the chair looking at her with the same ugly smirk on her face. Although Helena wanted answers to her questions, she was fully aware that there would be none forthcoming, unless of course her grandmother could see a way to cause more anguish. She was tired and cold and needed her bed but still she looked at the grandmother willing her to speak, hoping that death had mellowed her evil spirit. All she had to do was close her eyes and suddenly she was back in her own flat again. She awoke to find herself lying in her bed with the blankets wrapped around her like a cocoon. She lay for a moment or two before she got out of bed and wandered aimlessly into the kitchen. Her hand automatically reached out for the kettle and she flicked the switch. While she poured the boiling water into the mug, it suddenly dawned on her why her grandmother had come back; it was time for the fourth kill.

She was running out of ways to kill but the pressure building up in her brain screamed at her to find a fourth victim no matter how old. *No! I will not kill a child; even if the child is an offspring of my enemies. All Children are innocent.* She stopped dead in her tracks, the kettle still in her hand, suddenly realising why the grandmother had come back—she wanted Helena to suffer the ultimate horror—she wanted her to kill a child.

Lying on the couch in Klaus's office, a single voice penetrated the silence uttering the same cry over and over again. Klaus stopped writing and listened to Helena as she sobbed: "Go away and leave me alone. I won't do it, I will never do that, and you can't make me." Klaus watched as Helena seemed to wrestle with some unseen demon. Helena's head shook from side to side and her hands were clenched into fists of rage so tight that her knuckles turned white. The outburst ended as suddenly as it began and once more Helena was silent. Klaus moved closer to the couch and tried to hear what her still moving lips were saying. He stood and watched as her rapid eye movement told him that she was still not fully awake. He didn't know whether it was best to bring her out of her hypnotic state or to wait to see if she resumed her one-sided conversation with what he presumed was her grandmother. He stood for a full ten minutes with no discernable change so, she was brought out of the trance.

Helena did not respond at first but seconds later she opened her eyes so suddenly that she caught Klaus by surprise, he was leaning over her. She could tell by the anguished look in his face that he was concerned about something and she searched his face for clues as to what it could be. "What happened?" she asked, "Why are you leaning over me so closely? Something happened didn't it?"

Klaus instinctively stepped back, "I was trying to catch what you were saying," he said.

"What was I saying, what was that place you took me to?" She demanded to know every word she had said and to leave nothing out. Klaus hesitated before telling her almost word for word everything he had written down. She looked into his face when he had finished and said: "There is something you are not telling me. What is it?"

"I've told you everything, Helena. Do you want to see my notes?"

"No Klaus, but I can tell by your face there is something you have not said. What did I say that you don't want me to know?" Klaus could see that Helena was getting agitated and restless so, very quietly, he told her of the earlier outburst, as if she was being forced to do something that she didn't want to do.

"What was it?" Helena asked.

"I believe your grandmother wanted you to do something Helena. Can you remember what it was? It is really important that you try to remember, Helena." She thought for several moments, almost as if she was rewinding the tortured images in her mind. Slowly she nodded her head, looked Klaus in the eyes and said: "She wants me to kill a child. I told her I would not do it." Klaus

123

watched as her eyes filled with the tears of painful anguish. Taking a handkerchief from his pocket, he offered it to Helena. "We can stop for today, Helena; I think we have both had enough for one day."

Klaus gave Helena a few minutes to compose herself, giving him time to think about what he wanted to say to her. The state she was in he had to be very careful or she might react badly. Sitting on the chair next to her, Klaus asked Helena to sit on the edge of the couch. She swung her legs round and sat with her hands resting on her knees with her face looking down at the floor as if she were ashamed. She was afraid to look into Klaus's eyes. Taking hold of her hands, Klaus said gently: "I listened to you calling and you were in some distress, you were saying: 'I won't do it!' and telling someone to go away and leave you alone. Who were you talking to Helena? Can you tell me?"
Helena nodded slowly: "I was talking to my grandmother. She won't leave me alone and I'm scared of her. I am sure that the shadow and she are the same evil spirit haunting me. I wouldn't do what she wanted me to. Grandmother is still very angry with me." As she spoke the tears erupted once again.

"It is alright to let go Helena," Klaus said reassuringly. With the sound of his words in her ears her tears gave way to great sobs and to Klaus it seemed as if her heart was about to break. He sat beside her and gently put his arm around her shoulders allowing her to rest her head on his shoulder until the sobbing subsided. He knew it was not the right thing to do professionally, but as a compassionate human being all he saw before him was a young girl who needed the touch of another.

Eventually, the crying stopped but Helena was reluctant to move from the comfort of Klaus's arms. She looked up into Klaus's eyes and he could see that her ashen face was strained with fear and uncertainly. He was suddenly taken by a feeling that disturbed him, he tried to take his eyes away from Helena's face but, something told him to look deeper into her eyes and the sensation was irresistible. He could feel her breath on his face and he could feel the sensation changing into a stirring in his body.

*NO! This isn't going to happen!* Despite his determination, reinforced by his years of experience, he turned his face toward Helena and looked deep into her eyes. He was mesmerised by the look she gave him. She reached her hand up to his face and stroked it all the while holding his gaze and looking deeper into his eyes. Klaus knew that what was about to happen was wrong, but he was unable to stop himself. He moved close to Helena and was about to kiss her, at that moment she made the mistake of closing her eyes and he stopped himself just in time.

Helena was not to be denied; she thought she had done enough to capture him and she cursed herself for letting him slip away. Still she refused to turn her face away and she continued to look at his face in an effort to regain the advantage. Klaus was reluctant to release Helena from his arms because he was suddenly intrigued by the bizarre situation. It was a struggle of minds that he wanted to win. It had been a long time since he had been this close physically or mentally to a woman, so the challenge had other overtones. They sat together without speaking until a knock on the door broke the stony silence. The built up tension in the room was palpable and Klaus was certain that whoever was at the door would feel it. He managed to drag himself away and sat back at his desk before shouting: "Come in." A female officer was waiting to take Helena back to her cell and he felt reprieved, that woman probably saved his career.

Helena left Klaus's office and, as she did so, she looked back at him, gave a wan smile and whispered a quiet "Thank you," as she closed the door behind her.

Klaus sat in stunned silence in his chair for several minutes looking at the closed door through which Helena had just gone. He tried to file his torrent of thoughts into some semblance of order. *That could have been a disaster.* He lifted his heavy body from the chair and moved over to the window. A huge sigh escaped his lips as he realised, firstly, just how close he had come to being struck off, and secondly, how terribly lonely he was. Sitting with Helena in his arms had been the first time he had held a woman since his divorce three years previously and he was beginning to realise how much of life he was missing. Turning back to his desk, he collected his papers, turned off his lamp and left his office for the night. Tomorrow would be another day, how would he get through it? Something would have to be done that was the one certainty in his life…but what?

His walk along the darkening corridor was a long and lonely one and he did not look anywhere but dead ahead as he neared the exit. His thoughts were many and varied. He had no idea what the next day would bring but he knew for certain that his feelings toward Helena were changing. *Maybe it is time I took a few days off?*

Things were no different when he arrived home and thought about the situation all night. He knew things could not carry on and develop, he decided that something had to be done and quickly. If he didn't he might do or say something he would later regret. For now he had to keep things to himself, he had no family or confidante at work to talk things over with, so whatever he did he would have to work it through alone. Food was the last thing on his mind and his evening meal consisted of a few glasses of whisky—not the ideal way to plan a cohesive strategy but a welcome diversion. *What if things were different and I had met Helena under normal circumstances?* These questions were the nature of the thoughts invading his mind and the only thing that a whisky induced sleep did was to bring him dreams of a life with Helena.

Far away from the luxury of his suburban apartment, Helena lay awake in her cramped cell until the early hours of the morning; she knew that the mental virus that she had unleashed on Klaus was beginning to take the desired effect.

# Chapter Twenty Four

Klaus awoke the next morning with the mother of all hangovers. The amount of whisky he had drunk the night before had taken its toll. With the greatest amount of effort, he swung his feet out of bed and sat on the edge with his head in his hands thinking of the events of the past few weeks. Finally, he stood up rather drunkenly and walked naked into the kitchen to make a pot of strong black coffee, seeing as he couldn't face a breakfast it was the ideal remedy. He sat at the kitchen table, drank his coffee and smoked a cigarette, lazily blowing clouds of grey smoke into the air around him. He looked into the heart of the cloud and saw the face of Helena. *My God! This is the kind of thing my patients speak of in their lunatic ramblings.*

He drained the dregs from his coffee cup and took a hot shower. He took his time in getting dressed and as he did so he decided to read through the notes of his last session with Helena. There were so many details that at first he could not take in everything he had written. The page before him looked like a giant spider chart. Eventually some of them began to make sense and this in turn brought back memories of why he had drunk himself into a stupor in the first place.

He lowered his head and brought it to rest on the kitchen table, hands under his head placed as a pillow, and he wondered if he should go into the office that day at all. Conflicting thoughts crashed into his head telling him first to take the day off and relax to sort himself out. Try and forget that not only was Helena an attractive young woman, she was also a prisoner and a convicted serial killer. She was first and foremost, his patient and the thoughts he was having should not have even been considered. To begin with he is her doctor, secondly, he is almost twice her age; a man experienced in the ways of the world, and she is young enough to be his daughter; it would be almost like incest! But then again, conflicting thoughts came and told him she was not his daughter and, as long as they were discreet, no-one would ever find out about their relationship. Once again sanity waded in telling him that of course someone would find out eventually and then where would he be?

He had ludicrous dreams of spending the next twenty or so years with Helena, of sharing her life, her dreams, her hopes but most of all, her bed. He ran explicit scenes through his mind where he made love to Helena, of kissing her young and tender lips, lips that were begging to be kissed, of holding her in his arms and caressing her taut body. Try as he might, he could not dispel these thoughts. Then, in stark contrast, he began to think of the consequences of his actions should he be found out. Did he really think that this young, vibrant, beautiful and very sexy young woman was worth losing his job for? Or even worse—was she worth going to prison for? That was surely what would happen should the prison Governor find out—there are no secrets in prison for long. Klaus finally reached a verdict and decided what his answer was.

Back at the prison Helena was sitting in her cell patiently waiting for Klaus to send for her because she was convinced that he would. She usually spent at least one hour with Klaus every other day as he probed the darkest recesses of her mind. The mental onslaught of the other day would ensure that if anything, the sessions would be prolonged. All night long, she had lay awake in her bed with nothing but that thought running through her head. There were things she needed to talk to Klaus about, things that had nothing to do with her recovery. She had suspected for a long time that Klaus had feelings for her—after all he was just a man. She had begun to work on a plan months earlier that perhaps she could use this to her best advantage. She had to be patient and fully test the water before targeting him for real. She would know soon enough if her carefully laid plans were about to pay dividends. She began to doubt herself as the clock began to move desperately close to the time when she was to be escorted to his office. She forced herself to wait patiently but by 10 am there was still no sign of him.

*Perhaps these bastards have changed my schedule again just to raise my anger?* Helena was taken into the exercise yard for an hour each day, but because she was a category 'A' prisoner her schedule was changed randomly, sometimes three times in the same week. Here, away from her cell, she could think clear thoughts and she often reflected on what her life would have been like now were she not in prison. Shortly after 10 am, a guard came and took Helena out for her exercise. Helena asked the guard what time she was going for her session with the doctor. She was told to her horror that he would not be coming in that day. Helena didn't allow her face to betray her bitter disappointment. She didn't say a word as she walked into the exercise yard. She walked a couple of perfunctory laps before she sat in a corner on the ground with her knees drawn up to her chin and wrapped her arms around them. The guard looked on and shrugged, it was her time to do as she pleased so if she wanted to sit there for the hour she was welcome. Helena rested her chin on the top of her knees. The guard stayed at a respectable distance, allowing Helena her own space and time to reflect and, as long as she didn't cause any trouble she was happy to leave her be. The guard just wanted an easy life so who could blame her for not being the least bit curious as to her charges behaviour. She could sit there all day if it was up to her. As far as Helena was concerned the feeling was mutual, she just wanted to be left alone to come and go as she pleased into the land of her dreams.

Klaus had decided that it would help him and consequently Helena, if he took a much needed holiday, so he took the rest of the week off and went away for a few days. He needed time and space to get his head back into order and try to be the professional person he was supposed to be, not a hot headed fool taken in by a pretty young face. He also made plans for other changes, he began by deciding to cut the sessions with Helena down to two a week instead of the usual four to see how it went from there. That way there would only be twice a week when he had to control himself. He realised that he was walking on dangerous ground and he was taking big risks. He could so easily fall for her charms and he knew it would be professional suicide if he allowed that to happen. He had wanted to hold

Helena in his arms for so long and was just a second away from kissing her. *God knows what would have happened and how far it would have gone if that guard had not knocked on the door when she did.*

The week passed in a blur and all too soon it was time for Klaus to go back to work, he was physically refreshed but the question was, had he managed to pull his mind together? The last day of his holiday was spent in deliberations with himself as to whether he should hand this case over to someone else. That way he would be released from the prospects of seeing Helena again and things becoming even more diverse and complex. It was not the first time he had considered this and it would probably not be the last, but deep down in his heart, he knew he would regret passing her case over to someone else; besides that would be an admission of defeat, worse still incompetence. Someone else would get the pleasure and credit for Helena being either declared sane or insane.

It was with a heavy heart that Klaus awoke the following day. He lived a fair distance from the prison and he would usually drive, but on that day he decided to walk, just to give himself extra time for thought. Finally arriving at the prison gates he waited in the reception area and went through the usual search procedures before being given clearance to enter. So began another week, a week in which, he hoped that by the end of it, he would feel better about himself and he would have a definite vision of the best way forward.

# Chapter Twenty Five

Walking along the corridor that led to his office felt very strange to Klaus. Never before had he taken a holiday, in fact hardly a day off in the last 12 years. That had been part of the reason for the breakup of his marriage, too much time spent at work and not enough with the family. There had been ample warnings that it would happen but he had ignored them in pursuit of his career and when the inevitable happened the shock hit him hard. When his wife and family left the marital home Klaus threw himself deeper into his work and gleaned what little cold solace that reaction had to offer. That same kind of reaction that has driven so many professionals into the ground; in short, he was living on the edge and had been since his marriage break-up. Since that time he had lived on his own.

Half an hour and several cigarettes later, he pressed a buzzer and Helena was brought into his office. She stood just inside the door looking at Klaus with a smile on her face but Klaus simply sat at his desk looking at his notes. He did not even dare to raise his head for he knew that if he so much as looked at Helena he would be lost completely in the emotional maze that stood gaping before him

Helena's heart flipped in excitement, his refusal to look at her was the signal she wanted. Nothing else would have convinced her that she had made the perfect connection. In a dramatically slow movement, Helena eventually walked over to the couch and sat down. She sat for several moments, appearing to be subdued before eventually raising her head. She suddenly, without warning, turned and looked at Klaus when she sensed that he was looking at her. He quickly averted his eyes, but it was too late, he had been seen.

Several more moments elapsed before Helena realised that Klaus was not going to greet her with any form of attention so she lay on the couch and waited. Another stagnant pause filled the air between them with neither breaking the stony silence. This was a war of minds that both had to win.

*My God, she looks so innocent, so beautiful.* Klaus dismissed that thought from his mind and instead he manufactured the courage to walk over and sit on the chair beside Helena. "Are you ready to go back Helena?" he asked quietly. She nodded her head and within moments she was back in the familiar surroundings of her own flat.

She found herself sitting on the sofa looking blankly at the television. Although it was switched on, the screen before her might as well have been just an unfocussed haze of moving, swirling colour. She was deep in thought; it had been several weeks since the last killing and she had not had the dream. She began to think that perhaps the dream was not going to recur again—how wrong she was. That night the dream would return with a terrible vengeance.

Suddenly she was gripped by pangs of insatiable hunger. She almost ripped the door off the fridge to rummage through the combination of stale and decaying food. Her eyes were drawn to the slab of cheese that had grown an overcoat of green fur. Of everything before her, that was the most appetising. She placed it on the table and reached mechanically for the knife on the rack. As her fingers found their way around the blade a very different lust took hold of her being. She raised the knife high into the air and stabbed it down into the heart of her next victim…a lump of mouldy cheese! The thrill of power as the blade drove down through the cheese and into the wooden chopping board burned in her stomach. She was ready to kill again and only the death of a man would satisfy her hunger.

With the sound of bloodlust still pulsating through her ears the television suddenly burst into cohesion. She heard the name of her town being announced and she curiously walked through to the living room to listen. The announcement spoke of a regatta later that week. It was to be held on Saturday and was considered the highlight of the summer. There was usually a fete, circus acts, stalls of every kind and a great family day out. For the briefest of moments she almost allowed herself the luxury of slipping back into a good time in her own childhood. No! She dispelled the temptation to re-focus on the plans she had to make. The bustling crowds of the regatta would also attract young men on the prowl for young girls to seduce and one of those lucky young men was about to run out of luck forever. She showered and dressed in her most alluring outfit before she headed out onto the streets and in the Mardi Gras atmosphere she mingled in with the crowds as the throngs of people snaked lazily towards the river. She flung her arms happily into the air and moved rhythmically to the sounds of a dancing band somewhere up in the distance. She laughed out loud and marvelled at the outrageous costumes that passed her by swaying and singing. She was suddenly aware of a presence beside her and she turned her head sharply only to see the outline of a familiar face, it was the same young man who had been following her, she was certain of it. Her laughing smile changed into a frown because he had gone. *Perhaps I imagined him?*

The day wore on and soon the crowds thinned out leaving only the hardened, drunken revellers and the street sweepers who had suddenly appeared to clear away the mess. She searched the faces of the people who passed her by hoping to catch sight of the young man but it was to no avail, he had been there but she had lost him again. Wearily she headed home because the exhaustion of the day had driven out the lust for death that had seized her earlier in the day. *Still, this day was not for nothing, I was drawn here by the power that drives me to my destiny, he was here, I just know he was. I can feel him just as I could smell him. Perhaps he will be besotted enough, or stupid enough to want to find me?*

By 10 pm Helena was back in her flat and a feeling of total peace and serenity crept over her as she sat and ran the remains of the day through her mind. Curiously, and despite not finding her prey, she had never felt so good in a long time. Later tonight though, although she was not aware of it, she would feel as if she had been to hell and back, for who knows what the dead of night will bring.

On the stroke of midnight Helena let her body fall onto the bed but before she did she performed her usual ritual. She went around the flat checking all the windows and doors were locked, all the alarms were turned on and the lights were off. Shadows crept along the walls behind her in every room she entered, but she was blissfully unaware. Within a few minutes, Helena had fallen into a deep sleep; that is when the nightmare returned with a vengeance! From that moment on there would be no more peaceful sleep for Helena.

# Chapter Twenty Six

Helena slowly opened her eyes to find she was once again in the house of horror. She stood with her back to the same door but she had left the door ajar this time. Her grandmother was still sitting in the same chair and had the same malevolent grin on her grotesque face. Death had certainly not given her any of the peaceful serenity that can sometimes form the aura of a dearly departed. She looked as cold and ugly in death as she had in life. Before her grandmother spoke Helena reminded her that she would not and could not kill a child no matter what the consequences of her defiance might be. As the words left her mouth something moved on the wall behind the chair. Helena's eyes darted to the movement. A shadow appeared to detach itself from the wall and it stood just behind her grandmother.

*I might have known that evil shadow had something to do with this wicked bitch!* Helena watched, afraid to move, knowing that if she did so, somehow or other the shadow would try to stop her. Suddenly, her grandmother stood up and loomed like a gargoyle before her. Helena staggered backwards as she watched her grandmother grow until she was almost the height of the room. As she grew taller, she became darker and darker until she too, was like a shadow. She moved slowly to the rear of the chair and merged as one with the shadow.

Helena's face drained of colour as the shadow towered over her; she knew that in a matter of moments she too would be absorbed into the evil axis. She tried to turn her ashen face from the apparition but a tremendous force compelled her to watch. Her grandmother's eyes bulged in their sockets and her head turned a full 360 degrees with a sickening crunching sound that reverberated around the room. She raised her hands in a dramatic sweep like a masked executioner might raise his bloody axe and the severed head after the deed. Helena stood paralysed as her grandmother's arms began to envelop her. Suddenly the door slammed shut so hard it made Helena jump and the force of it made the house shudder. The shock of it lifted her bodily from the floor and she collapsed into a heap. She closed her eyes waiting for the blow that she knew was about to crash into her skull. The blow did not come; instead the room filled with what sounded like the voices of the damned. It started as a low, rumbling growl and quickly grew into a deafening roar. She lifted her eyes to her grandmother as an irresistible force began pulling her into the centre of the room. She tried to struggle free but it was hopeless, when she reached the centre of the room the force relented and she suddenly stopped. She could feel her grandmother's piercing eyes burning into her. A pain shot through Helena's head like a bolt of lightning, it was so intense she wanted to vomit but still she couldn't take her eyes from the glare of her grandmother. The pain continued until Helena finally began to understand. She was not going to be allowed out of that room until she agreed to her grandmother's demand.

Summoning every ounce of her mental strength Helena managed to lower her head until she was looking at the floor which had started to swim with the throbbing in her head. She knew that her grandmother could do with her as she pleased yet still she hesitated. She was playing games with her. *Maybe she is looking for some kind of evil compromise?* Would Helena be able to think of another way, a way she would be able to kill again but not kill a child? She realised she was going to have to think and think quickly. *There has got to be some connection between her getting stronger and the killings I am being compelled to do.* The droning sound in the room began to lessen and Helena realised that her grandmother's strength was beginning to fade. Helena raised her eyes again to meet her grandmother's and she saw that she was looking agitated. Helena could see that something strange was happening. Her grandmother had moved back towards the wall. She watched as her grandmother reached out her right hand to the window, and as her hand touched the glass the window turned into a mirror into the real world. Through the mist of her eyes Helena could see herself in a park. There were lots of children happily playing while parents sat in groups chatting and enjoying the sunshine. Her grandmother turned her head to Helena, and her eyes bore into her head forcing her to look deeper into the mirror. Tears began to run down her face as she followed her grandmother's outstretched hand pointing to an innocent young boy. Helena's head shook back and forth as she sobbed: "I can't do it grandmother. I won't kill a child. Please don't make me do this." The whole house shook as her grandmother's eyes widened into a terrible, blazing stare. Her voice penetrated into Helena's head as she hissed: "If you do not do as I say, you will suffer a fate worse than that inflicted on me."

Helena stumbled backwards in shock and slumped limply against the wall behind her. She looked up in dazed confusion and blinked the moisture from her eyes.

"You will do as I say you worthless bitch!" Her grandmother's venomous voice echoed through the room. Helena opened her mouth to answer but no words would form in her parched mouth. Her burning throat betrayed her again as she tried to let her grandmother know that she was beaten. All she could do was nod weakly and her grandmother smiled that familiar grin of evil satisfaction. In her mind, Helena was running the lines of her defence: *I have no intention of carrying out your twisted commands and I would rather die myself before I do that, but if I can get from this evil place then I will tell you anything and make you believe it.* Helena dragged herself to her feet and stood swaying before the fading image of her grandmother. She melted into the wall until only the shadow was left, that too disappeared a moment later. Helena could never have known that the shadow was about to take on a life of its own again and follow her every move. If she had known…she would have done as she was told.

It was 2 am when Helena woke up so suddenly that, at first she could not remember where she was. She sat up and instinctively her arm reached out and turned on the bedside lamp. She looked wildly about her until she realised that it had all been a horrible dream. It took several minutes for her to finally realise that she was alone, at home and in her own bed. Only then did she relax and let her head rest against the wall behind her. She let out a huge sigh of relief but she also knew that there would be no more sleep for her that night. She got out of bed and walked sleepily into the bathroom. She splashed water onto her burning face and looked at her ghoulish reflection in the mirror. Her hair was tousled and matted from sweat and her face was ashen. She opened her eyes wide and saw the web-like capillaries were bloodshot and bruised. She looked and felt a total mess. As she combed through her hair with her fingers, she looked at her reflection and made a vow that, no matter what her grandmother did to her, she would not kill a child. Maybe, if she completed the fourth kill very soon, just maybe, it would be enough to appease her grandmother's ferocity, for a short time at least. In that short time Helena would have time to find a way out...that was her plan anyway.

# Chapter Twenty Seven

Helena stood in the bathroom and shivered, whether it was from the chill in the flat or from fear, she did not know. Walking into her bedroom, she put on her bathrobe and walked through into the kitchen. What she needed was a cup of coffee she needed to think and, most of all she needed to be rid of the grandmother. She was being hounded and began to wonder if committing suicide would be a better option for her. It took an hour of serious thought for her to realise that even if she did commit suicide, there was no guarantee she would be rid of the grandmother. *At last, I am beginning to think straight, if and when I do get rid of her, there will be purgatory or hell between us!*

By 3.30 am, Helena was dressed and contemplating the prospect of perhaps going out. At that time of the night it was hardly likely there would be anyone around and walking always helped clear her head and organise her thoughts into a cohesive order, an order that she could understand at any rate. Despite the slim chance of meeting another living soul she decided to take a knife with her anyway. *Better to be prepared.* Besides, it was pointless going back to bed because sleep was as distant to her now as her ruined childhood. Back then she could sob herself back to sleep but now, her eyes had run dry. Wrapping herself up in a coat, gloves and a scarf around her neck to keep out the chill, she unlocked the front door. Gently closing it behind her, she looked up and down the street. There was no-one around and all was in complete darkness. There were no lights in any of the windows, no moon or starlight, the only lighting was from the street lights. Because of the darkness, Helena was not aware that she was being followed, not only by the shadow but also by the young man from the park. *Is this really happening or am I back in my nightmare?*

Kurt Muller is a man of 30 years of age but the 'thought lines' as he called them on his forehead might suggest that he was older. He stands about 5'8" in height, and has neatly trimmed brown hair. His slender build belies a well toned, muscular frame, pretty average one might say and nothing outstanding, that is, until you see his eyes. They are big and brown and seductively inviting, they express a knowing calmness and a depth of worldly wisdom, so many attributes that a member of the opposite sex could find instantly beguiling. He tends to dress casually most of the time when he is not working. Because of his gentle and quiet manner, very few people, on seeing him, would have taken him as a policeman. He had been on his day off when he walked into the park fully intending to sit and read his book to relax a while in the sunshine. Helena had walked into the park, sat down close by him and fate decreed that Kurt would not be opening that book today.

From the very first time he had seen Helena in the park, Kurt had become intrigued by her. Her appearance, her manner and her looks had all left their impression on him and made him wonder about the woman herself. He wanted to know who she was, where she lived and what she did so, on his days off, he took to making sure that he put himself in the places she might be likely to visit. At first he struggled with the idea that some of the criminals he had arrested had started off possible romances innocently enough, following a girl they are smitten with and after the rejection the following quickly descended into the ugliness of stalking and intimidation. This girl was different, he could recognise the signals that she was aware of his interest and she liked it, why else would she appear *randomly* at places he might be? He was painfully shy and would never approach her outright but if he could find her address he might find an excuse to call. Eventually he found out where she lived and the next part of his romantic plan was about to be put into operation.

That night, he stood in the darkness of a doorway across the street from Helena's flat. He had been there almost an hour just watching, not thinking for one minute that he would see her. He was just about to go home when he saw her door open very furtively and she left the flat. Instinctively he pressed himself against the door back into the shadows and hid as she looked up and down the street. He watched her step into the street and head off in the opposite direction. *What on earth is she doing?* Like most good officers of the law his police training was ingrained into his being, he was never off duty. He didn't think for one moment that she had any criminal intentions but he didn't think it was a safe thing to do for a beautiful young woman. *What do I know? She may have an early start.* Still, he felt compelled to follow her at a discreet distance to make sure she was safe. Her step was determined so he deduced that she had a definite destination. The only thing he hoped was that it was not some midnight tryst with a secret lover...that would ruin everything. Sticking to the shadows he watched her go into the park and sit on a bench. His heart sank; *Damn it! She must be waiting for someone.*

It didn't take long for his sudden heart wrench to turn more into curiosity. Half an hour later and Helena was still sitting in the same place. He knew he couldn't stand there all night because that would amount to stalking. He watched for another few minutes as he deliberated. The sky was beginning to lighten in the eastern horizon so he was satisfied that she was in no imminent danger. He crept back through the shadows until he was clear of his footsteps being in her earshot and he made his way home. If he had stayed for just a few minutes longer he would have seen Helena leave the park by a different exit. She had walked almost another mile when she found herself heading back home. The walk was pleasant enough and the quietness of the night helped her to relax and clear her head, for a little while at least.

She was perhaps a mile from her home and the break of dawn was about to send its first rays into the hearts of the morning chorus when she noticed a figure up ahead. As she approached she could see that he had probably been sleeping rough in the park, she wasn't afraid because of the way he appeared to be shuffling rather than walking, he would pose no physical threat to her.

"Good morning," he said in a gruff voice.

Helena took pity on him, "Good morning to you sir," she smiled.

"Could I trouble you for a few coppers to buy an old soldier a morning coffee young lady?" he said automatically thrusting out his hand.

She looked into his eyes as she stopped to hand him a few coins; there was something familiar about him but she couldn't figure out what it was. As she held out the coins he brought up his fist and caught her with a thunderous blow to the side of her head. As the blackness of unconsciousness filled her head completely he took hold of her dazed and falling body and dragged her easily into the park. Helena knew what was happening as if she was looking at the scene from outside her body, but she was powerless to stop it, she was completely at his mercy. Flashes of her grandfather's childhood assaults came flooding back, she was in no doubt what he was going to do. The effects of the blow were beginning to wear off but she was still far too weak to fend him off. Through the haze of her regaining consciousness she could feel her body being lifted, she made the mistake of opening her eyes and the madman punched her in the face again. The blow was only a glancing blow and delivered with nothing like the venom of the first punch so she pretended to be unconscious. She waited for him to begin the agony of him ripping her clothing from her.

In his eagerness to finish the deed he pushed up her coat and Helena felt the weight of the blade in her pocket. She could hear the urgency in his rasping breath as he tore at her underclothes. The years of abuse at the hands of her grandfather had taught her how to keep a clear mind in a situation like this, she had long since learned to separate her mind from her body and she was about to put that experience to devastating use. Her hand slid into the pocket of her coat and her fingers expertly clasped around the handle. Looking down for an instant at the vile monster she smiled inwardly. *Go on you old bastard, do your worst!* He was so intent on ripping her clothing from what he thought was her unconscious body that he paid no attention to any movement she made. He tore at her last piece of underwear and moved his legs up to sit astride her so that she would have very little room to move, she was completely at his mercy...from the waist down. Now he was ready to take his time, he moved his hands all over her body, touching her most intimate places. She waited until this vile man dipped his head to put his mouth to her breast and she chose that moment to take the knife fully from its hiding place.

The ferocity with which she plunged the knife into the man's back, made him sit up and stare at Helena. The look of shock on his face made Helena smile. He clenched his fist in readiness to punch Helena again when the blade went up to its hilt into his chest. A deep gurgling sound came from his mouth as he half coughed, half choked up a mouthful of dark red blood that looked almost blue in the gathering dawn. His body made one final jerk before he fell dead on top of her. She easily pushed him off her by rolling his shoulders and he fell to one side. The violence and eagerness of his attack had given him strength above his weight and as he rolled onto his back Helena could see that he was thin and dirty and that his frame had been padded by layers of collected clothing. She lay on the grass looking at his face that was already turning into a pale, grotesque death-mask. All her clothing was in tatters and she was covered in his blood. The only part of her clothing that was intact was her coat which she pulled around her. She got shakily to her feet and looked again at the body; she suddenly had the urge to mutilate it. Her face was throbbing from the force of the blow and she thought that perhaps her jaw was broken. The pain however did not stop her from kneeling down beside the corpse and slicing off his penis. She opened his mouth and put it inside. *Choke on that you bastard for the rest of eternity in hell.* She gathered up her ripped clothing and stumbled home in the early dawn, the knife once again hidden in her pocket.

Whether her grandmother was pleased with her or not, the fourth kill had just been completed. It was not a planned kill so Helena did not feel quite the exhilaration she had on the previous occasions but she still felt good as she reached home and closed and locked the door behind her. The time was 5 am and the sun was steadily rising by the time Helena showered the blood from her face and hair; the birds broke the silence of the morning almost in unison and Helena smiled as she climbed into bed with a feeling of satisfaction. The man's mutilated body would be found in the park at some point during that glorious morning but Helena was confident in the knowledge that there was nothing to connect her to the murder...or so she thought.

## Chapter Twenty Eight

The morning dawned bright and sunny. It was almost 11 am before Helena finally awoke to the sun shining like a rapier through the gap in the curtains. She stretched her body to its full extent and let herself relax again; she smiled as she recalled the unexpected fortunate events of the night before. She threw the duvet off with a determination that the day was going to be a good one no matter what life threw at her. As her feet touched the warmth of the floor she noticed what was left of the clothing she had worn last night dumped in a bloody heap on the floor. She picked up what was left of her under skirt and examined it. She remembered very clearly the events of the early hours of the morning. The smile on her face faded as she realised that, although she had carried out the fourth kill, she knew in her heart that her grandmother would not be pleased and would return to vent her anger. The other problem rapidly brought to the fore of her mind after a glance in the mirror was the nasty bruising and swelling to the whole of the left hand side of her face. She lifted her fingers to the skin and winced as she prodded the swelling. Her earlier thought that perhaps her jaw was fractured was supported by the shooting pain that shot through her face. *I can't go to hospital with this; I will stay indoors until I can mask this bruising and take the swelling down.*

At approximately the same time as Helena awoke, there came an unearthly scream from the vicinity of the park. A young woman was taking her baby son for a walk through the beautiful surroundings of the park in the sunshine. Her baby was happily gurgling away to the sound of his mother's voice when he suddenly became aware that his mother had stopped walking. There was a strange look on her face. They had turned a corner of the path and there, lying in full view of everyone, was the partially clothed body of someone who had obviously been murdered. The woman stood in shock as the colour instantly drained from her face. First there was a soundless scream, which was quickly followed by a scream loud enough to be heard from anywhere in

145

the park. She began to laugh hysterically at the sight of so much blood and the obvious signs of mutilation. The knife lay bloodied and guilty on the grass beside the body. The eyes stared lifeless at the sky and the blue, grey pallor of his skin made it obvious that he had been there for some time.

In his office Kurt Muller was about to take a mid-morning break when his telephone burst into life. Someone had reported a possible body being found in the park and it was down to him to follow up if the uniformed boys found the report to be accurate. It wasn't long before they confirmed the finding of a body in suspicious circumstances. He had been deep in thought when the initial call brought him out of his reverie. He put on his jacket as he left the office and made his way to his car. He arrived at the scene to find the area already cordoned off and the young woman who found the body was being calmed and spoken to by two women police officers. Forensics arrived more or less at the same time so he waited for them before he approached the actual murder scene. Looking past the woman who was being comforted by the female officers he saw the man's body lying just off the path with the green grass discoloured by the pool of drying blood around the corpse.

"Is that the lady who found the body?" he asked one of the officers.

"Yes sir," the officer replied with an air of efficiency. "We knew you would want to keep her near."

"Yes but you could take her away from the immediate area, the poor lady is obviously in need of a seat," he said.

The officer looked about her inquisitively, "There aren't any seats here sir,"

"How did you get here?" he asked.

"In our patrol car sir," she answered questioningly.

"Well there is your first clue; does it have seats in it?" he said. Muller turned to his colleague from forensics, "Can't get the staff these days." The officer turned away in embarrassment and led the lady to the patrol car whilst the other officer wheeled the confused baby off in the same direction.

Kurt followed the young woman to the patrol car to talk to her as the forensics team began going over the murder scene. The quicker she was questioned—especially before the shock had time to take its full negative effect—the better. After just a few moments it was clear that apart from giving her name and address she was in no condition to give any kind of worthwhile statement. He made sure the officers had her name before he told one of them to drive her home. Before he let the car pull away he took hold of the car radio and called headquarters to officially confirm the murder and to try to draft in extra man-power to keep the already gathering media at bay. *The last thing we need is any evidence being trampled beneath the feet of a great horde of snappers and amateur gumshoes.*

Forensics examined the body and at first all they could see was the stab wound to the chest and of course the missing penis. By that time Kurt had arrived back at the scene and was taking a close look at the body. The wound in the chest was probably the killer blow because the forensics team already guessed that the relatively small amount of blood from the severed penis suggested that it had been cut off after death. The post mortem would of course confirm it. As the body was turned over the other wound to the back became obvious but again it was guessed that it was not the killer blow. The knife was gathered from the grass near the body and put into a plastic bag; that would be tested for fingerprints and its possible source of purchase. The only thing which didn't add up was where the severed penis was?

Kurt had worked alongside the forensics team for a long time and he had great admiration for Helmut Wiess the man examining the area. Weiss called Kurt over as he looked transfixed at the ground. "We may not have the killer just yet, but I think we can safely narrow it down to sixty per cent of the population," he smiled.

"Now I will be impressed if you can tell me exactly which sixty per cent that might be," Kurt said following Weiss' gaze.

"Well then, prepare to be impressed, our killer is female," he smiled again.

"How can you be so sure?" Kurt asked.

"Because I know what made these holes in the grass, it was the heel of a woman's stiletto heeled shoe. There is something not quite right though and that will need further deliberation."

Kurt shook his head slowly, indicating that he was baffled. "And what might that be?"

Helmut pointed to the configuration of the footprints. "These large, heavy prints belong to our friend here, would you agree?"

Kurt nodded, "Yes of course I would."

Helmut moved his head closer to the ground, "Well my dear fellow, by the look of the female footprints, it appears that they only walk away from the scene."

"So what are you saying?" Kurt asked.

"I am saying that the murdered man appears to have carried his killer here."

Kurt looked down at the murdered man's open eyes and pointed. "Why would he do that?"

Helmut smiled, "Now that is for you to find out detective."

Back at Helena's flat—and despite the pain in her face— she was completely unaware of anything but an overwhelming sense of peace and happiness. It was only later when she tried to eat she found that the swelling in her face and worsening pain meant that she couldn't open her Mouth. She needed to get help soon or she would starve to death. *How did I allow myself to be attacked like that? He caught me completely off guard.* She berated herself for allowing it to happen in the first place. She went over in her mind exactly what had happened in the time leading up to her attack and she began to think if there were any clues that she could have left behind that would lead the police to her door. Suddenly a series of sickening doubts began to filter through her head. *I know I left the knife behind, but they can be bought anywhere in the town, but did I leave anything else.* She looked over again at the heap of bloodied clothes and realised that instead of just dumping them into the bin she would have to pick her way through them to make sure that nothing was missing. The very thought of handling the clothes that such a vile creep had touched made her feel sick. She held her hand up to her face again to try to ease the pain and it was then she saw that one of her fingernails was broken. She quickly covered her hand as if averting it from prying eyes. There was nothing else for it; she had to venture out back to the park to see for herself if the body had been discovered. She was just about to open the front door when she heard voices on the other side out in the street. It was the sound of two women talking about the latest body to have been found and that it was particularly bad because it had been found near to the children's play area. Helena pulled her hand from the door and slumped against the wall. Now she would never be able to rest not knowing if a policeman was about to turn up and arrest her.

An incident room was being set up at the scene just as Kurt was leaving to go back to his office. He knew there would be a barrage of questions from the press and he wanted to brief his commander in person before the vultures descended. His boss was his usual supportive self. "You have twenty four hours to wrap this one up or I want to know why."

Kurt rolled his eyes at the familiar statement which preceded every case he had ever worked on. He knew that his boss meant he had to say all the right things to the press. The press had been invited to attend a scheduled press conference at 3pm; Kurt looked at his watch and saw that he had time to go to pathology to see if a report was ready. The last thing he wanted to do was give the press the opportunity to question his competence and so panic the general public. He jumped into his car and drove the short distance to the city mortuary. The pathologist was just finishing his report when Kurt walked in.

"Do we know what killed him," he asked eagerly.

"He choked," the pathologist said with a deadpan expression on his face.

Kurt had known him long enough to know that he had a wicked sense of humour but he was in no mood for games.

"I have a battery of snappers out there waiting for me to tell them that everything is under control and you want me to tell them that he choked?"

The pathologist lifted up the man's severed penis and laughed, "If you had this baby in your mouth, wouldn't you fucking choke?"

"You mean…" Kurt stuttered.

The pathologist put it back in the kidney tray, "Yes we found this in his mouth, and no, he didn't choke, he died from the stab wound to his stomach. The wound in the back was not deep enough to have killed him but the one at the front would have killed him in seconds, right through his ticker, bull's-eye; he was dead before his head hit the ground. Kurt turned to leave, he had heard enough.

"Hey copper," the pathologist called after him, "Do you want to know how his cock got into his mouth?"

Kurt knew there was a punch-line coming but he had no choice but to fall for it. "Go on then, if you really must. No, let me guess, he was eating a frankfurter supper in his lap and he lopped the wrong one in half?"

The pathologist shook his head, "Nice try, but way off the mark, his cock was forced into his mouth by a woman, and it was an aroused cock just before it was severed."

Kurt's face took on a serious look, "How do you know?"

The pathologist lifted up a pair of tweezers. I know it was forced into his mouth because the woman who did it lost this fingernail against one of his teeth. And I know he had a hard-on as he died because of the amount of blood still in it."

"Can you tell which finger the nail is from?" Kurt asked.

"Hey I'm a pathologist not a clairvoyant buddy," he shrugged.

Kurt laughed, "If only things were that easy, I don't mean the exact finger it came from I mean can you tell if it is right handed or a fore finger."

"I wish I could tell you whose it was but it might help to know that it looks like a middle finger of a woman's right hand."

Kurt looked at his watch, "I have to be at a press conference in ten minutes, could you have a full report on my desk later today?"

The pathologist smiled. "I will have it with you within the hour; I know the old man is putting you under pressure."

With that Kurt left and headed to his meeting with the pack of baying wolves.

Helena paced the floor wringing her hands not knowing what she should do. She was certain she had left no tell-tale signs on the man's body. She lifted her hands in front of her face and, after looking at them, she decided to cut the fingernails making them all the same length then no-one would suspect her. She sighed as the thought crossed her mind that she was safe and she was worrying over nothing. *The old bastard is dead and he deserved it.* After almost wearing a hole in the carpet, Helena stopped pacing the floor and began to calm down. She reasoned that no-one had seen her near the park and, so what if they had. She was young and free and was no danger to anyone how could she be suspected of anything? She gave herself a good telling off for being stupid, if she did as she planned and remained indoors until her injuries healed than she would be totally in the clear.

Helena could not have been aware that Kurt Muller had in fact seen her in the park at precisely the same time as the murder occurred. She was not aware either that despite the work he suddenly had thrust upon him she was not very far from his mind. No matter how he tried to separate the two things he was forced to admit that she had to be called in to be interviewed. His main problem with that would be in explaining how he knew that she was at the park at that hour of the morning. She had to be spoken to and eliminated and that was that.

The press conference was every bit as awkward as he knew it would be. Questions were fired at him from every angle, questions that he knew he didn't have answers to. One well known craggy faced reporter brought out the public panic element and that really set the cat amongst the pigeons. From that point on it became such a negative free for all that the chief of police put a stop to the conference.

"Why don't you people do your job and allow us to do our job?" he barked in frustration.

"Our job is to report the facts and you haven't given us any," one reporter shouted.

"A man has been murdered and it will be just a matter of time before the perpetrator is brought into custody. That's all you need to know and that's all you need to print. We have doubled police presence on the streets on a twenty four hour basis so the public are absolutely safe," the chief of police answered, "Now that will be all ladies and gentlemen." With that, the police entourage filed out of the conference room and the collated media were left to pick the bones out of his comments to make their headlines.

Kurt went back to his desk and read the pathologist's report. The image of a woman emerged from the printed words and moved like a mirage in front of his face. No matter how hard he tried he could not picture any other face on the mirage than that of Helena and he didn't like it, in fact, he hated himself for it. His immediate dilemma was, did he take along a detective to question her officially—which would open up another can of worms—why should he be questioning an apparently random woman? Or did he stake out her apartment and continue with his secret surveillance? Eventually he chose the latter option.

# Chapter Twenty Nine

Stefan Prem sat reading the murder headlines of the newspaper in his lap. *That evil bitch is behind it, she has struck again. It is time I made my move before the police close the net on her and take her away from me. That bitch is mine.* He was sitting not half a mile away from the very spot where Helena had tried to kill him. As far as Helena knew Stefan was dead; she had killed him with a single knife thrust to his abdomen and buried the blade so deep that she couldn't pull it out. Helena had always thought that their first meeting at the bus was a random thing but Stefan had known her as a child growing up in the same area and going to the same school as her. She was always a weird kid who kept herself to herself and she had no interest in boys whatsoever so had taken no notice of the boys in school. Everyone in their hometown knew the story of Helena and how her parents had been killed and the terrible night that Helena had murdered her grandparents. He had heard the rumours but he could never be certain if they were simply gossip. Either way it was of no interest to him, he had been obsessed with her from the very start and he was determined to have her. The fact that she had almost killed him only heightened his desire. He thought that he could be her saviour and that she would grow to love him and together they would live a fairytale life with children and a little place in the country. Even the blade he kept as a morbid souvenir of their bloody romance could not convince him that her only interest in him had been to see him dead. He would have her at any cost but if he didn't act swiftly then she would be gone forever.

When the bodies of men began to appear lying on the streets of town and in the sewers, he began to put two and two together and came up with the one conclusion that he was not her only victim and that Helena was responsible for their deaths too. The thought that she had seduced them made his skin crawl and he was glad that they had paid the ultimate price for defiling her pristine body.

Once he recovered from his wound he had set himself the task of finding a way to *haunt* Helena. He set about it with stealth and dogged determination; she would be made to suffer the height of mental anguish before she became his slave.

Helena believed that there were now four men dead because of her, Stefan intended to keep it that way for some time yet but he had to come up with a way to stop her soon otherwise she would be caught and their life together would be finished.

His plan had been to occasionally allow her to catch a brief glimpse of him before he disappeared and melted into the crowds. He was always careful to choose his moments well; firstly, to have the maximum negative psychological on her and secondly to make good his escape. She would think she was either going mad or just seeing things.

The one thing he was regretful of was the time they had spent together. He sat recalling their lovemaking and how special that was but when the thoughts kicked in that he meant nothing to her the sentimentality soured into vengeance. *Now* was the time to make himself known to her once again. Slipping her lock had been a piece of cake; he was surprised how easy it was for him to gain access into what should have been a fortress. He waited until darkness before he slipped silently from his flat, walking quickly in the direction of Helena's home.

Before long he was in the street of Helena's flat, furtively he looked around blissfully unaware that the shadowy figure in the dark saloon car was leading the murder hunt and on high alert for anything remotely suspicious. Kurt crouched down as he watched Stefan walk towards Helena's gate. He was suddenly confronted with a dilemma, here he was watching what he thought was the home of someone that he had seen in the vicinity of the murder and a man appears on the scene acting as if he could be up to no good. Did he call for back up and risk blowing everything or did he wait it out to see what happened. He had a sworn duty to catch the killer but he also had a duty to protect Helena. And as a policeman he had every right to stop and question anyone who was acting strangely. Finally he decided to wait and let the scene roll before he made any sort of move. Stefan opened the front gate and looked around before he walked up to the door, his plan was to break into her flat by slipping the lock and write a message to her in blood that his ghost had returned from the dead. She would wake up in the morning and see the message and it would push her to the brink of insanity. The time would then be ripe for him to take complete control of her mind by showing her that he was indestructible. She would have no choice but to become his captive bride.

Suddenly a group of late night revellers appeared at the end of the street and made their way noisily towards Helena's flat. Stefan had no choice but to wait until they passed before he tried the door. As the revellers neared Helena's flat her light went on and Stefan was forced to back away into the street, he couldn't risk her seeing him before he was ready.

Kurt had also seen the revellers and Stefan's reaction to them; it was all he needed to convince himself that the stranger at the door had questions to answer. He decided that he would follow him. He waited until he was well away before he got out of the car and hugged the shadows on his trail. Stefan had been spooked by the sudden appearance of the revellers so he decided to call off his mission for that night in favour of returning the following night, everything had to be perfect and that included his entrance into her flat. His plans for the following night would include waiting until there was absolute silence of the night before he slipped the lock and entered her flat.

While Kurt was following Stefan, Helena sat alone in her flat having been disturbed by the noise in the streets; she began thinking over the events of the past few days. By then she had calmed down enough to think rationally of what her next step should be. There were plans that had to be made and put into effect. As far as she was aware, there were now four murders completed. If she had been aware of the goings on between Kurt and Stefan she would not have dared to leave the safety of the flat. As it was, she decided that within the next few days, number five would have to be accomplished. After all; what better time to strike again than when the whole town was in a state of near panic, with everyone suspecting everyone else?

Helena realised that she had not eaten for the better part of a day. All day, she had not moved from the sofa, but had sat curled up in one corner going over in her mind everything that had happened recently. She came out of her reverie at the noise out in the street to discover that the room was dark and cold. She stretched her arm out and put on the lamp as she looked tentatively over at the window just in time to see a shadow go past. Stefan could never have known but his presence at the flat that night had indeed had the desired effect, his shadow passing the window as he moved back into the street had done as much to un -nerve Helena as his original plan. With her hands trembling, her eyes darted wildly all around the room and only when she was sure that there were no other shadows around, did she move from the sofa and into the bedroom. That night, the dreams returned with renewed force.

# Chapter Thirty

Klaus sat in his chair at his desk once again going over the notes written at his last session with Helena. It had been almost an hour now since she had been taken back to her cell and Klaus had watched her leave his office. He ran his hand through his hair to help gather his thoughts before he dropped his head in his hands. He tried several times to read and reread the notes he had made but, as it stood, he could make neither head nor tail of any of it; it just didn't make sense. *I need a break from this.* Pushing his papers to one side, Klaus stood up and, leaving everything as it was, he decided he had had enough for one day. All of this could wait until tomorrow, he was going home.

Klaus had left his car at home that day and he was thankful for that, the walk home would help him to clear his mind or make sense of his jumbled thoughts. He plodded along with his hands deep in his pockets his thoughts spinning in his head; the main thought was of course Helena. Try as he might—including some of his own therapeutic remedies—he could not get her out of his mind. Everything about her, her voice, the way she looked at him and the way she moved, everything added to his torment. He was a man trained to subdue his feelings in order to remain focussed with his patients but he knew well enough that Helena was aware of his growing feelings for her. Klaus finally arrived home and as he went through his front door the emptiness of the house hit him like a hammer and he knew he had to do something soon otherwise *he* would go crazy. He poured himself a stiff drink and he flicked half heartedly through the morning papers. It wasn't long before he laid back and closed his eyes.

Helena had been escorted back to her cell after the latest session with Klaus. She sat on her bed with her knees brought up to her chin and her arms wrapped around them. She looked straight ahead of her at the wall as a deep sorrow welled up from the very core of her being. It was sorrow for her lost childhood, sorrow for the men she had killed, sorrow for herself but most of all, sorrow for Klaus. She knew in her lonely heart, that Klaus loved her but, in his position there was nothing he could do. There must be some way she could help him. She lay on her bed and fell into a deep sleep for the first time in weeks with no dreams invading her night.

The following morning, Helena awoke with still no idea on exactly how she could help Klaus. Their next session was to be in two days time, so she had plenty of time to think of something, after all, he was about to become her lover and that's what lovers do for each other, they ease each other's suffering. She was not yet aware that Klaus was already preparing plans that would settle all his confusions in one go. Helena eagerly waited for the day of the next session. She was going to make sure everything went right and, if she was lucky, she would hold Klaus in her arms, pleasant enough thoughts to send someone to sleep in the hope of days to come.

Two days later, Helena walked into Klaus's office with a sweet smile on her face, a smile that radiated hope for the future. After closing the door behind her she looked at his ashen face and realised that he hadn't slept for a long time. He was unshaven and dishevelled to the point where she almost didn't recognise him. The smell filling the air was of stale whisky which Klaus must have consumed in large amounts for it to linger so badly. Helena walked mechanically to the treatment couch and sat down. She wasn't even certain that he was fully aware that she was in the room. *You are trying to fight this my love; why don't you accept that to be as one is our fate?* She wished with all her heart that she could somehow find the courage to express the words running through her mind like lovers running hand in hand along a golden beach.

She could not believe the changes she saw in the man sitting in front of her. She wanted to reach out and stroke his troubled face to reassure him that she was his for the taking. Where was the man so confident that he could help her put her life back together and help her to start all over again? Who was this imposter, this wreck of a man lost to everything but the bottle of whisky? She was at a loss as to what to do. The minutes waiting for Klaus to speak seemed like endless agonising hours, she had tried to speak to him several times with no reply. She knew that Klaus would get into trouble for turning up for work in a state like that but if he didn't respond properly soon she was going to have to ask for help. She walked back to the door all the while keeping her eyes firmly on him. His cold, desensitised eyes followed her and she had just put her hand on the handle when she heard his muffled voice asking her to wait.

He raised his head from the desk and looked at Helena. She could tell by the deep red circles around his eyes that he had been crying. She walked back to his desk and she saw without a doubt why he was this way, his feelings for her clearly showed on his face. Helena knew what she had to do; it hit her like a great epiphany, that night she would begin to make her plans but for the time being she had a session to get through so that her guards would not suspect anything. She took the coffee percolator and poured a mug to offer him. He looked up with a glazed expression on his face before he lamely held out his hand. She stood over him to make certain that he drank it quickly.

Although he was not fully sober, he was soon capable of getting through this final session of the week. Helena went back to the couch and lay down, that was the signal that he should begin the session. He got shakily to his feet, adjusted his tie and jacket and took up his familiar position to the left of the couch with his chair just behind Helena's head. Somehow he eventually began the session and once again Helena was taken—despite his condition—expertly back to her own flat where she was lying in her own bed getting ready to drift off into a deep, deep sleep.

# Chapter Thirty One

That night, Helena was sent in her dream back to the alley where now only two doors remained. She stood in front of the white and blue doors and wondered which one she should take this time. Although she knew that, no matter which door she chose it would ultimately lead her to horror, she was also aware that the longer she took to decide which door, the longer the horror would last. Eventually, she chose the blue door. Tentatively she edged her way to the blue door, all the time wondering what ghastly fate awaited her. Hesitating slightly, she stood with her hand on the door handle turning it until she heard the click and the door was open.

Hesitantly stepping through the open door she was at first reluctant to release the handle because that at least offered her a modicum of comfort and a possible chance of escape. A sudden pain shot up her right arm forcing her to let go of the handle. *My god, the evil games have started already!* She watched as the door closed behind her and vanished leaving no way out. She was left standing in the middle of what appeared to be a field. At first glance, there appeared to be one single tree about three hundred yards ahead of her. It was obvious that the tree had some relevance so she had no choice but to walk along the path towards it.

From a distance there was nothing other than the tree before her but soon two statues made of stone had seemingly risen from the ground. Looking closely at their faces, Helena was aware that they looked very much like two of her murder victims and her blood ran cold. She couldn't take her eyes off the statues as she walked slowly toward them. She got to within a few feet when she stopped dead in her tracks. The faces of Stefan and the man from the park were staring at her. Her dreams were often bizarre but no matter how hard she tried she could not fathom out the meaning behind the statues. *Does it mean that Stefan is now immortalised, or does it mean that his killing will immortalise me?* She walked around behind the statues to avoid their deathly stare but wherever she went, the eyes appeared to be following her.

It was not so much the statues that troubled Helena, but if they represented her victims—or one of them at least—why were there only two instead of four; and why these two particular men, one dead and the other very much alive? Suddenly, as she stood looking transfixed at the statues, it dawned on her. The man from the park is alive and well, but Stefan is dead. *Am I being offered a way out of this mess by choosing either a life of madness or lasting peace in death?* Desperate to find the subliminal meaning she ran her mind back in time to when she murdered Stefan. She recalled in vivid detail how his body fell to the ground as she walked a little way into the alley. She also remembered that when she returned, his body was nowhere to be seen. She had always believed he had crawled away into the sewers and became food for the rats but, what if he hadn't? *Surely no one could survive those injuries…could they? What if Stefan is still alive?* To Helena, the thought was simply unbearable.

Helena decided to challenge the urges in her body to make any further approach to the statues; instead she sat down on the grass behind them to avoid their stare. *If they want me they can damn well come and get me!* In a show of fearless defiance she dared them by shouting at them to come and get her. As she sat on the grass a curious thought began to emerge. *What if the statues are trying to tell me that neither of the men are actually dead? That would explain a multitude of strange goings on in my apartment lately.* She recalled the times when she found the open windows when she had been certain she had closed them and the heart-stopping sight of Stefan standing in front of her. Surely everything that had happened had been just her imagination working overtime. There was no way that Stefan could still be alive, it was impossible. Slowly rising up from the grass, she steeled herself, certain that when she took a close look at the statues their true meaning and identity would become apparent. With renewed courage she approached the statues again.

It didn't take long for her fear to return with a vengeance, brought on by the sight that met her. The statues were no longer ahead of her. They had somehow moved and stood several yards behind and to the right of her. They had taken up positions in the shade of the only tree in this strange land. In a state of near panic

161

she looked all around her, but there was no-one else in sight. *Who could be playing these evil mind games? Is it you grandmother?* Yes the statues had moved but she sensed that it was by a force of great evil. She stood rooted to the spot and stared at the statues waiting for their next trick. She knew that the evil was about to reveal itself, and all its heinous intentions, she was nothing more than a frightened rabbit caught in the headlights of an all-powerful juggernaut.

The force manifested itself in a blinding revelation, she finally realised that it meant that Stefan was still alive somewhere out there. The statues were a message that she had to find him and the man from the park and both of them had to die—two statues, two men, two deaths, both at the same time. As yet, she did not know how she was going to do it…the evil was compelling…there had to be a way.

The driving, searing pain that began to carve its way into her burning brain became intolerable and she sank to her knees in agony. Despite the pain she had to think clearly and come up with a fool proof plan but, first of all, she needed to rest…she needed to sleep. The stresses of the day both in her conscious being and in her hypnotic state had taken their toll and she was too exhausted to think of anything. Something told her to sleep so she lay down under the shade of the tree; she closed her eyes and instantly fell into a deep sleep. She awoke two hours later to discover she was back in her flat and lying in her own bed – and very confused by the latest events made so startlingly real by her terrible nightmare.

# Chapter Thirty Two

Helena was wide awake, of that she was quite certain, what she was not certain of were the images of her dream as they re-emerged in her head. She still lay in her bed in the familiar surroundings of her own flat. She rested her head against the headboard and thought of the night's events, trying to pick her way through the relevance of it all. She began by re-examining the two statues and the conclusions she had reached in her dream but she could still not come to terms with the fact that Stefan was still alive. Her heart sank when she realised that it meant only three kills had been completed, and it meant that she was going to have to kill Stefan all over again along with the man from the park. That would explain why the evil spirit of her grandmother was angry with her.

She became aware of a distant voice calling her name and realised that she was still in Klaus's office and he was in the process of bringing her out of the trance. Once she was fully awake, she began to tell Klaus of the fears she had at that time when she realised that Stefan had not died at the first attempt. She looked as if she was far away in a world of her own as she recalled the immense amount of pain he must have been in. She told Klaus of the two statues in the field how she had taken it to be an evil portent from her grandmother that she had to complete two kills at the same time. She told him of the statues looking like Stefan and the man from the park. She pleaded with Klaus: "Please, you must help me. I know it was my grandmother who sent those statues and made them deliberately look like Stefan and the man from the park to tell me that I had to kill again. You have to help me to stop her from making me do it."

"I can help you to fight her, but you have to let me fully into your life," Klaus said calmly.

"I don't know what you mean. You are my only hope and you are in my life, you have my sanity in your hands. What else must I do to let you into my life?" she sobbed.

Closing his notebook he said: "For now Helena, you do nothing but rest. I will let you know what you have to do and when." Helena smiled inwardly as she left his office that day because she knew her trap was closing in on him and he did not have the faintest idea.

This was the last session for the week and Helena was escorted back to her cell. She sat and thought about that last session. Earlier, when Klaus had put her in the trance, he had not realised that she was not fully under. She had felt his fingers as they gently brushed over her lips. She had felt the silent tear drop onto her face and she felt Klaus wipe it away as he tried, without success, to control his emotions. She heard his voice as he quietly told her that he loved her and that he did not care if she had killed all those men, all he wanted was to spend time with her. She knew that he was no more mentally stable than the people he was supposed to be treating. He would pay for his transgressions in a way that he could never imagine.

Sitting alone in her cell, Helena was by now fully aware that she had successfully manipulated his mind into loving her despite their worlds being a universe apart. I too am deeply in love for the first time in my life and I will find a way to make it happen between us. Love was sitting alone in his office along the corridor and she could do nothing for the time being, but she knew that all it would take to make him completely hers was one more turn of the mental screw.

She was to discover what her eventual fate would be the following week and she had a sneaking suspicion what that fate would be. A smile spread across her face as she thought about the growing possibility of Klaus sharing the rest of her life not as her doctor but as her bewitched lover. She fell asleep with thoughts of Klaus filling her head and the possibilities for the rest of her life with him.

That night the dream returned but with a little more subtlety. There was no shadow or noise, in fact, there was hardly any indication that it was the same dream. It had begun ordinarily enough in an amusement park and gently led her through the dream until she was standing in the field once again looking at the statues, only this time the white door was also visible.

She was just about to discover what the white door signified when she was suddenly awoken by the sounds of doors banging and raised voices running along the corridor outside her cell. Her head was still in a daze as she got out of bed and stood with her ear against the door to hear what was going on. Strain as she might she could not gather enough of the odd words she heard to be able to put together what was going on, but she knew that something was very wrong, it was then that she heard the name…Klaus. *Ah! Another poor soul in need of his services; well you can forget it because he is mine!* She walked back over the cold stone floor and climbed back to bed. Minutes later, everything was quiet again and once more silence reigned.

# Chapter Thirty Three

The next morning Helena awoke with an unshakable feeling of dread deep in the pit of her stomach. She had slept soundly and, at first, could not recall having been woken up at all. It was only later that morning as she was being taken for her exercise that she remembered the commotion in the corridor and quietly asked the guard what the noise had been last night.

"No talking!" the guard snapped back at her, "You know the rules."

"But I have to know," Helena pleaded.

"The only thing you have to know is that if you say one more word you will spend the next month licking the wounds of the beating I give you."

*I hope we meet again on the outside, bitch, I will make you beg me to kill you.*

Helena knew when she had overstepped the mark and decided to use other methods to find out what went on the previous night. As the guard took her back to the cell in silence she put her hand in her back as the cell door opened and she pushed her violently into her cell.

"If you must know what happened," the guard sneered, "You will have to find a new doctor to listen to your whimpering in future, because our glorious doctor Klaus has killed himself."

Helena staggered backwards beneath the weight of what she had just heard. *No! This can not be!* The utter shock and horror was too much to comprehend. She was lost—what was she going to do now? Silent tears erupted from the core of her being as she slumped down into a corner of her cell and wept uncontrollably. Her one true love was gone forever and she had not even had the chance to tell him of her feelings for him. Her mind games had gone too far and he was dead, killed by the unbearable thought that their forbidden love could never be consummated.

The guard stood peering through the spy hole in the cell door watching Helena and wondered why she should be so distraught; after all, he was just her doctor...wasn't he?" She thought it was time to find out why she was so upset. She opened the door and went inside; her large frame filled the doorway. She walked over to Helena and saw that she was blinded by tears running down her face.

"Why the outpouring of such emotion?" she asked coldly.

"Even people like me can feel compassion," Helena said, "But that is something you will never understand."

The guard drew back her boot and kicked Helena hard in the stomach.

"People like you can feel my boot and that is the only thing you need to understand, you murdering bitch."

The guard kicked her again before she turned and locked the cell door again. Helena's tears of loss turned into tears of rage as she clenched her fists and hammered the heels of her hands against the floor.

She had gone through so much over the past few months that, by then, she was mentally and physically exhausted. She curled up in the corner determined to retain the vomit that was rising in her throat, she didn't want to give the guard—who was still glowering at her through the spy hole in the door—the satisfaction of seeing her degrade herself. The guard closed the spy hole and left Helena alone with her grief, genuine or contrived. Helena eventually cried herself to sleep and in that sleep she found herself in her own flat, sitting on her own sofa with her feet curled under her.

She was acutely aware that very soon she would have to make her plans for the double murder. She had no idea where to begin—what she did know was that it was going to be very hard work, much harder than the previous murders. She rose slowly from the sofa deep in thought and walked over to the window to close the curtains. Still in her thoughtful mode, she reached up and took hold of each curtain and looked straight into the face of Stefan. He was standing outside the window staring back at her with a sickening grin on his face. Helena screamed in shock and fell away from the window, when she looked again Stefan was gone.

Was he real or was it another figment of her over tired imagination? She collected her scattered senses and went through to the kitchen to grab a carving knife. If he was in her imagination then he would be gone, but if he was real, then his presence was about to solve one of her immediate problems. She returned with the knife and carefully opened the window, she searched everywhere but, there was no one in sight. She closed the window and made doubly sure that it was locked securely before she closed the curtains. She held the knife close by her side as she moved toward the sofa where she sat down. Still trembling from the shock of seeing Stefan her thoughts were spinning around in her head so much it was beginning to hurt. *How many times over the past few weeks have I seen Stefan?* She began to rationalise that every time he had been seen, he was either around the flat or out in a crowd where either way he could make a hasty getaway. The suggestion was that he was indeed alive and not just imagined.

She had to find a way to kill Stefan and the man from the park, and she had to do it in such a way that it would not arouse suspicion against her; there was no more room for mistakes. Even if she had to tear them limb from limb, she would make sure that they were dead! That night Helena went to bed with ideas running around her head, ideas of how to kill them and how to dispose of their bodies. Suddenly sitting bolt upright in her bed, she realised that there was still a chance he lived in the same flat he had when they were together. *Why of course, why didn't I think of that earlier? If he is now stalking me, I can turn the tables on him.* She decided that the following morning she would go to the flat and watch until he or the current occupier ventured out. *Then we will see just who is driving who to the brink of insanity!* She pushed the kitchen knife under her pillow before she drifted off into a dreamless sleep.

The following morning Helena was awake before dawn and she was in no mood to waste one second of her day. Within the hour she was armed and ready to leave her flat for her day of secret surveillance. She planned to leave home just after 6 am as she reckoned that Stefan would not have left the flat by then. She wrapped her scarf around her face to conceal the bruising and she walked into town. She crossed over by the end of the park to the block of flats that Stefan had lived in. She bought a magazine and sat on the bench beneath the trees lining the area opposite the entrance. With her scarf and shades no one—not even her closest associates would recognise her. Stefan had lived on the fourth floor and from her position she could not tell if the movement of the curtains was him or the present occupier, but one thing was certain, someone was in that flat. She had read and re-read the first page of her magazine a dozen times before her patience paid off, but things were not as clear cut as she might have imagined. Stefan did indeed leave the flat, but he was accompanied by another man. She could hardly believe her eyes or her luck when she looked at the other man…it was the man from the park. They were obviously deep in conversation making Helena realise that they knew each other well. *Enjoy that conversation because it is going to be your last.* Things were unfolding far better than she dared imagine, she had come to find one victim and found they both lived in the same apartment block. She would deal with the man from the park later—first, she had to deal with Stefan. With them safely taken care of, her grandmother would leave her alone…that was what she believed anyway.

# Chapter Thirty Four

Giving the two men plenty of time to get well away, Helena entered the block of flats carefully making sure that she was unnoticed. She still held a key to Stefan's flat but, instead of using it, she quietly lifted the letterbox and listened for any noises inside. *He may have a woman in there.* When she was certain that the flat was empty she drew the key from her pocket. Helena was just inserting it into the lock when she heard raised voices at the far end of the corridor heading her way. As there was nowhere for her to hide— and she hadn't prepared an answer for if a security guard were to ask what she was doing there—she quickly unlocked the door and stepped inside. She closed the door and stood with her ear pressed against it listening for the voices to pass by. She held her breath as the voices rose in volume and faded again into the distance. She moved away from the door and stood in the living room. She let her eyes wander around recalling all the happy times she had spent visiting here. It was a modern flat and well kept to say it was a bachelor pad, he obviously had a penchant for tasteful interior design but by comparison to the décor it was sparsely furnished. Helena made herself focus on the job in hand, which was to find a way to be rid of Stefan once and for all.

Forcing herself to concentrate, she moved around the flat allowing her hands to roam over the furniture. Finally reaching the bedroom, her eyes rested on the bed where she and Stefan had enjoyed so many passionate nights. All thoughts of sentimentality were driven coldly from her mind; her only thoughts were on finding a way to kill the man who had avoided death to become her tormentor. She left the bedroom and walked into the kitchen. To the right of the sink was a cupboard where both the gas and electric supply meters were kept. The sight of the meters gave Helena a sudden burst of inspiration; she knew exactly what to do. She looked in the drawer where the cutlery was kept and saw a bread knife with a serrated edge. *Perfect!* She saw a box of matches next to the cooker which would make an ideal detonator. She peeled the striking paper off the box and ripped it in half. Then she sliced the heads off half a dozen matches. She cut off the sulphur and placed it delicately between the two halves of the striking paper. Going back to the cupboard, she hesitated for just a minute before using the knife to make a small incision in the pipe allowing the gas to escape slowly. *By the time he comes home this place will be thicker than fog.* She went to the front door and carefully inserted the detonator between the door and the frame. When the door opened the sulphur would spark and hopefully the whole flat would ignite. Mission accomplished, she let herself out of the flat, walked down the stairs and out of the building. Crossing the road to the park, she sat on the same seat where she was still within view of the flats; she sat down, casually opened her magazine... and waited.

It was just after five in the evening when Stefan and the other man arrived back at the building. They walked into the block of flats without noticing the young woman on the bench opposite. The feeling of excitement within her grew as she knew they must be nearing Stefan's gas-filled flat. A moment later...BOOM! A huge explosion ripped through the flat and took the best part of the top floor with it. Helena could hardly contain her delight as she watched the blaze take hold before she walked away, content in the knowledge that Stefan and the man from the park had been blown to pieces.

She arrived at her own front door and, with a smile on her face, closed the door behind her. She rested her back against the door and allowed her body to relax. With a song rising in her throat she prepared a late supper and took it with her to sit on the sofa to watch television for the rest of the night. The last newscast of the night was reporting an explosion in a block of flats in which two unidentified men had been killed and an elderly woman from a nearby flat had died from a subsequent heart attack. *Oh well, planning a death like that is not an exact science.* A news reporter stood in front of the ruined block of flats and Helena could see the devastation caused by the explosion. The reporter said the police had ruled out foul play. *A perfect murder!* She was very proud of what she had done, and content to know that this could never be traced back to her.

It was not until several days later that the news emerged that the two men killed in the explosion were Mr Stefan Prem and off duty detective Kurt Muller. Helena was in her kitchen preparing lunch when she heard the news and walked into the lounge with the knife still in her hand. She could not believe her ears, *Kurt Muller, he must be the man from the park.* She began to panic, not because of Stefan's death but because she had killed a policeman. *Perhaps this would make them look again at the suspicion of foul play?* She ran over her movements leading up to the explosion and was satisfied that nothing she had done or failed to do could incriminate her. It took a few moments for her to calm down enough to realise that she had not been seen, so surely there could be no evidence to tie her to the explosion.

# Chapter Thirty Five

That night the dream had returned with a feeling of almost serenity. Helena had no hesitation in going through the one remaining door. She closed the door behind her, and as usual, it disappeared. The only thing standing in front of her was a box. When she opened the box, she found at the bottom, a doll made of sticks and it was wearing ragged clothes, it looked like the effigy of a man. She did not understand its meaning but she gathered it up and put it in her coat pocket.

Two weeks passed and Helena thought that the media coverage of the explosion would have subsided. The bruising on her face had cleared enough for her to venture out without her disguise. She felt the need to visit the sight of the blast to put her mind at ease. As usual, she carried in her pocket the knife—just as extra insurance, and her hand was wrapped tightly around the handle. Instinctively she looked around making sure she was not being watched before she walked toward the block of flats. All the residents had been moved out of the block so it was totally empty and Helena would have no reason to be too cautious. The outside of the building was being photographed by several ghoulish sightseers so she paid them no attention. Keeping both hands in her pockets, one on the knife and the other on the stick man, she pushed open the door and entered the block. She realised she still had one man to kill so she wanted to be ready in event that the opportunity should arise. It came sooner than she thought.

If Helena had taken a little more time and had been a little more vigilant, she would have seen the solitary plain clothes policemen watching her from a distance. His instructions from his superiors were not to go near anyone entering the building but to contact them immediately. He watched as Helena entered the damaged building and he dutifully alerted his superiors. His instructions were to wait until back-up arrived to take over. If the person left the building he was to follow at a discreet distance. Within minutes it looked as if the whole fleet had been mobilised.

Police cars and motor cycles of all shapes and sizes—all silent and without their lights flashing appeared on the scene.

Helena was totally unaware that she had been seen or of the commotion that was going on out on the street. When the media reported the blast they had in fact been working in co-operation with the police and several details had been omitted to make the killer think they thought it was just a freak accident. When Kurt Muller had followed Stefan on the night he had seen him lurking outside Helena's flat he made himself known to Stefan. Under questioning he had told Muller that he intended to wreak a savage revenge on the woman who had almost killed him. In return for his freedom, Muller recruited Stefan to help him snare Helena before she could commit her next murder, without his help there was no evidence to put her at the scene of her latest crime. Somehow they had to lure her out of her flat so that they could catch her in the act. Muller had instructed his staff to set up surveillance cameras inside Stefan's apartment block. Stefan would then *appear* to Helena. She would then be compelled to re-visit his former flat to see if he really was alive or dead. Yes the plan was a long-shot but under the circumstances it was worth a try. Everything had worked like clockwork…until the unexpected explosion. Despite her disguise Helena could not cover the fact that a female had entered the flat on the morning of the explosion and the police had it all on film despite the blast. The whole thing was captured by the surveillance van that Muller and Stefan had used and which the police found after the explosion.

A sound behind Helena made her turn around and she found herself face to face with a tall thin man. He had a dark brown moustache and a small goatee beard. His eyes were a deep blue and his hair a dull mousy brown which looked as if it had not been washed in months. His clothes appeared to be all tattered and torn with haphazard patches sewn into the knees and elbows. His shoes were almost falling off his feet with holes at the front where the tattered leather barely covered his toes. Helena and the tramp stared at each other locked for several minutes without moving.

Helena was the first to move, backing away to stand with her back to what was left of the window with the tramp moving toward her. The look in his eyes was one of starvation and not only of food but also of the comfort only a woman can provide. Seeing Helena he had been unable to stop himself and watching his eyes made Helena fully aware of his intentions. She was determined this would not happen again and her hand tightened around the handle of the knife. She was concentrating so hard on the man in front of her that she failed to hear the police enter the building and slowly make their way up what was left of the stairs.

Without warning, the tramp lunged at Helena. Her eyes widened in fear as he made a grab for her hair and pulled her down onto the floor among the debris. He began tearing at her clothes and Helena finally found the voice to scream. By the time the police got to the top of the staircase, Helena had buried the knife into the neck of the tramp and she was covered in his blood. Kill number six—and totally unplanned was complete.

Helena scrambled to her feet and stood looking at the still jerking corpse with her back to the door. She was still unaware of the police standing behind her until a pair of irresistibly strong hands caught her and pulled her arms behind her back. Handcuffs locked into place and at last Helena Maria Shultz was finally secure. The look of relief on Helena's face spoke volumes, the killings were over and so were the dreams. Although the policeman was not aware that the woman standing in front of him was responsible for six murders, he was clearly aware of the tramp lying dead in front of him and he knew he had been summoned to the scene as part of a major police operation.

Kept in handcuffs, Helena was transported back to the police station and questioned. The story that unfolded was far more than the police had hoped for. All the details of the previous killings she was responsible for emerged and the police had no doubt she was telling the truth. In all the previous killings, certain details had not been released to the media and Helena told everything. As she spoke with clarity and confidence she knew that everything she said was being recorded and this would eventually be used against her when she appeared in court. She simply didn't care; she had lived through the cruelty of a thousand lifetimes so a court of law held no fears for her.

Eventually Helena was duly charged with and pleaded guilty to six murders. She was taken to a woman's prison where she was held on remand to await sentencing. Part of being in prison for her crimes, requested that she be seen by a psychiatrist to determine whether she was or was not insane. This process began shortly after arriving at the prison. The day arrived when she would learn her eventual fate.

Whilst waiting to be taken to court, Helena sat in her cell reflecting on everything that had happened in her short life. The only thing she really regretted was the fact that Klaus had committed suicide because of her. Soon she was taken by two burly police officers up the stairs to a waiting police van where she was transported back to the high court. She stood in the dock with her head bowed and her hands by her side. The judge placed the black cap on his head and calmly said "Helena Maria Schultz, you have been found guilty of six counts of murder. The sentence of this court is that you be taken back to prison to await execution. At that time you will be hanged by the neck until you are dead. That is the sentence of this court and may God have mercy on your soul.

As Helena stood on the gallows she was asked if she had any last words. The hangman stood in awe as she smiled and said: "My grandparents made certain that my mind was never going to be my own. They are now rotting in Hell but I will soon be free to live with Klaus forever in eternity."

## Other Titles From Cauliay Publishing

**Kilts, Confetti & Conspiracy** *By* Bill Shackleton
**Child Of The Storm** *By* Douglas Davidson
**Buildings In A House Of Fire** *By* Graham Tiler
**Tatterdemalion** *By* Ray Succre
**From The Holocaust To the Highlands** *By* Walter Kress
**To Save My father's Soul** *By* Michael William Molden
**Love, Cry and Wonder Why** *By* Bernard Briggs
**A Seal Snorts Out The Moon** *By* Colin Stewart Jones
**The Haunted North** *By* Graeme Milne
**Revolutionaries** *By* Jack Blade
**Michael** *By* Sandra Rowell
**Poets Centre Stage (*Vol One*)** *By* Various poets
**The Fire House** *By* Michael William Molden
**The Upside Down Social World** *By* Jennifer Morrison
**The Strawberry Garden** *By* Michael William Molden
**Poets Centre Stage (*Vol Two*)** *By* Various Poets
**Havers & Blethers** *By* The Red Book Writers
**Amphisbaena** *By* Ray Succre
**The Ark** *By* Andrew Powell
**The Diaries of Belfour, Ellah, Rainals Co** *By* Gerald Davison

### Books coming Soon

**Underway, Looking Aft** *By* Amy Shouse
**The Bubble** *By* Andrew Powell
**Darkness of Dreams** *By* Pamela Gaull
**Minor Variations and Change** *By* Graham Tiler
**Spoils Of The Eagle** *By* Alan James Barker
**The Trouble With Pheep Ahrrf** *By* Coffeestayne

Lightning Source UK Ltd.
Milton Keynes UK
07 September 2010

159522UK00001B/90/P